This Year's Ghost

This Year's Ghost

Michael Chin

JACKLEG PRESS

JackLeg Press
www.jacklegpress.org

ISBN: 978-1956907179

Library of Congress Control Number: 2023945776

Other books by Michael Chin

You Might Forget the Sky Was Ever Blue

Circus Folk

The Long Way Home

My Grandfather's an Immigrant, and So Is Yours

Stories Wrestling Can Tell

Praise for This Year's Ghost

In *This Year's Ghost*, Michael Chin builds each story from the cleverest of premises—ghost subscription service! life without dogs! boys made of stone!—sinking readers immediately into not-quite, just-off worlds and then moving us beyond cleverness to insight, truth, love. I admire especially Chin's tender balance of charm and sincerity. This collection will haunt me, and my fiction-writing classroom, for ages.
—Jennifer A. Howard, *Flat Stanly Reports to His Third Grader* and *You on Mars: Failed Sci-Fi Stories*

Michael Chin examines everyday relationships and emotions through the lens of fantastical, unexpected, and often deeply strange situations—reframing the struggles of adolescence in a world where children are made of stone and glass, transforming the pain of first love and lost friendship through a tale at clown college, and asking what someone who can access all the answers in the universe would truly want to know most. *This Year's Ghost* is a surprising and insightful collection that will leave readers unsettled in the very best way.
—Tara Karr Roberts, *Wild and Distant Seas*

A triumphant collection of stories by a writer whose strong vision balances the darkness and light of our modern world refreshingly and enchantingly. *This Year's Ghost*'s worlds of puzzles and heartbreak may often contain fantastic beings and futuristic technologies, but they capture the ubiquitous need for connection and affirmation at the core of human experience. Michael Chin is a highly transportive writer whose other books should move to the top of your queue immediately afterwards.
—Jason Teal, *We Were Called Specimens*

While the plots of these wildly imagined stories will captivate the reader—a company that rents out ghosts; a teenager who has a crush on a girl made of glass; a slot machine where you bet on a percentage of the life you have left—the real magic is in Michael Chin's ability to go beyond a story's premise and deliver insights about identity, love, and loss. These weird and wonderful stories will enchant and enthrall, while sneakily delivering a dose of insight and humor.
—Susan Jackson Rodgers, *This Must Be The Place*

For my mother

Contents

This Year's Ghost

The installation guy was curiously normal. You sign up for a subscription service to have a ghost deposited in your home each year, you expect a monk in dark robes, waving candles and chanting from holy texts. But there he was—a portly kid dressed in khaki coveralls, a nameplate that read *BUD*. He reeked of cigarettes and looked too young to be so balding. The kid gave off the aura of somebody who'd set up your cable or kill cockroaches.

"You do a lot of these?" I asked him by way of small talk. I was never good at small talk.

He nodded along, adjusting the knobs on a little black box. I'd learnt from my Terms and Conditions manual that they were *containers* to keep my ghost on the premises. I was under strict directions never to move them. The list of rules unfurled from there, like never asking about the afterlife my ghost came from and never asking them to communicate messages to other ghosts. A mix of eerie and legalese, punctuated with a warning any violation of terms would result in a lifetime ban and litigation.

"A lot of widows want their spouses back." Bud moved my two-foot fiber-optic Christmas tree aside to get a box flush in a corner. "Especially around the holidays."

I'd meant my question about the service and its popularity, but the fact I belonged to my own sub-category of cliché customer confirmed I wasn't on the cutting edge of anything about this process. This Year's Ghost was tried and tested; spooks probably haunted half my neighbors already.

A year must have seemed like a long time for younger people. A year's time, you get fired and hired someplace else. You move. You meet a pretty girl and start talking about moving in with her. When you're young, a lot can change in a year.

The installation process was anticlimactic. It didn't take long, a little apartment—living room, kitchen, bathroom, my bedroom, the guest room I'd speculated my sister might come to stay in sometime. More space than I needed to myself. Not much space at all.

Bud announced I ought to see my wife within the next forty-eight hours, left me a copy of my service agreement, and was on his way.

#

That night, I found Lucille at the stove. Sensible enough, because that's where she spent most of her waking hours, albeit at our old house, not this apartment. She wore mom jeans and a pastel pink blouse. She seemed at ease until I said her name.

Her hair stood on end. You'd think I was the ghost the way I scared her.

The reading I'd done had told me something like this might happen. Some ghosts get requested a lot and know the system. Catch them on their first go-round, though, when they first arrive, and it's disorienting. The odds are they don't remember dying the way the living don't remember falling asleep.

Lucille was angry with me.

"What'd you think?" She passed her hand through the handle on the oven door and then went straight for my face, unable, of course, to lay her hands on anything. "Did you think I'd like this?"

I told her I'd missed her and wanted to see her again, and I was sorry I hadn't considered how she'd feel.

"You *never* think," she corrected me. "You're so selfish."

One of the points all the This Year's Ghost literature was fuzzy about was *how* a ghost would come back. It seems to vary. You might get the ghost of somebody in the prime of their life. You might get them the same way they'd left the mortal plane. Somebody on the forums speculated it was however the ghosts thought of themselves.

Lucille? She looked a lot like she had, maybe not at the very end, but not far from it—maybe her last year. She'd been unhappy with me for a while. If we'd married in a different era, or later in life—less inertia weighing us down—we might've split up.

We spent a lot of those first weeks of her ghost year startling one another, in no small part because she'd appear and disappear in ways neither of us knew how to anticipate. I grew certain I'd made a mistake and looked up the cancellation policy. Lucille caught me looking and we fought.

Then things got nice.

I was rereading Steinbeck on the toilet when Lucille materialized in the tub. The scene started awkwardly, but also reminded the both of us better days, before we had a big TV in the living room, and it was a simple pleasure to read to one another, and even more so in a hot bath. So after I'd flushed and cleaned myself up, I filled the tub with hot water and dipped in. We sat at opposite sides of the tub, my material limbs interlaced with her phantom ones. Probably a trick of rippling water, but I swore I could feel her there. I read aloud.

This would give way to the two of us sitting at the dinner table together. I always ate more than her anyway, and she'd sit and make conversation—her doing so in ethereal form wasn't so different from nursing a glass of Cabernet while I continued to chow down. Then we'd alternate choosing what we'd watch on TV at night, like we had for years, and I remembered some of the small kindnesses associated with having a partner around the house—if not the most romantic pieces of a marriage, at least the companionship. Wasn't that what I'd wanted out of This Year's Ghost?

Around the ten-month mark, it dawned on us Lucille's time was running out. What started in offhand comments and speculation returned to a familiar conversation from her final years in corporeal form. "What do you think will happen when I go away?"

Of course, I should've expressed more concern, but I was my pragmatic jackass self when I reminded her, she'd already died long ago and didn't seem so bad off.

She asked me if I'd use This Year's Ghost again, and I should have said I wouldn't, but I wasn't strategic or sensitive enough there either. When I made mention I had queue, she grew obsessive with asking who else was on it—which of my jackass old drinking buddies, or if I'd honestly want my mother coming to live (or be dead) with me for a year?

When she asked if I were going to bring back old girlfriends, I should have cut her off. Not only denied it but changed the subject to the celebrity options This Year's Ghost made available. Or I might have steered us away from ghosts altogether, and talked about traveling back to Europe, or finally making it to Hawai'i for a vacation.

But I hesitated, and Lucille picked up on where my queue was headed.

The only secret I did manage to keep in those miserable last weeks: Lucille wasn't my first choice at all. I'd wanted Dorothy Houston.

#

Dorothy was the one who got away. An actress with Broadway ambitions, a voice like an angel. I'd sat through a community theater production of *A Christmas Carol* to support her—just a chorus member—in those first months we were together. She wore an old-fashioned blue dress that fit like a potato sack, but even so, she was a beauty.

In the end, she was too cool, too smart, too kind—a little too much for me, and in such obvious ways that, in retrospect, it wasn't any mystery why we hadn't worked. She'd gone steady with me for nearly a year, though.

One of our first dates, I brought Lucille to see *A Christmas Carol*, two years after the first time I'd sat through it. Dorothy wore the same dress. She hadn't aged a day. I watched her exclusively each time she was on stage and considered hanging around after the show to say hello and congratulate her on the performance but thought better of it.

I've long suspected losing out on Dorothy was a big reason why I moved so fast with Lucille in the aftermath—not so much that *we* were ready to settle down, as I was ready after having had my great love story.

I found Dorothy's ghost occupied that first year, and so my queue would defer to my second choice, Lucille. I reasoned it was probably better I got out some of the kinks of cohabitating with a ghost anyway. Lucille was good for that.

#

I say all this so you'll understand my disappointment when the next service agreement revealed I'd have the ghost of my mother installed.

Mom struggled like Lucille those first days, with the quandary of what to do with herself in non-corporeal form. Moreover, while Lucille'd only missed a couple years on earth, Mom had nearly twenty to catch up on and had such trouble wrapping her head around smart phones or streaming television. She refused to believe Donald Trump was president and wouldn't trust the news websites I showed her either. I had to buy newspapers for her.

It took Mom longer to get settled in as a ghost, sure, but we had fun reminiscing about the old days. I filled her in on my sister Susy (retired to Florida) and how my brother Jim had passed away peacefully. Mom had the bright idea of having Susy visit for a weekend and they hit it off easily, chattering about everything in ways that underscored my own inadequacies as a conversation partner. When I drove Susy back to the airport, I asked if maybe she'd sign up for This Year's Ghost and have Mom stay with her after my year was up.

"A whole year with that woman?" Susy's voice was sharper, like I'd remembered it from our teenage years. "I don't know how anyone could stand it. I liked seeing her, though. I appreciate you having me, Chuck."

I don't know if it was Susy's comment or the sheer passage of time, but Mom started grating on me, with her nagging about leaving dirty socks on the living room floor and listening to the television too loudly.

I removed Dad and my grandparents from the queue, lessons learned.

Mom had always liked cars. She said Dad's fascination with cars was the first thing she'd liked about him, and she spent long summer afternoons watching him work beneath the hood of one jalopy after another, fetching him Budweisers.

Her last days with me, she sat by the window facing the road watching the cars drive by, humming to herself when she liked the look of one, and going so far as to whistle when a vintage red Thunderbird rolled past.

#

My next ghost was Maurice, a poker buddy from back in the day, and maybe an oddball choice for such a high spot in the queue. I got a kick out of seeing his name, though, and remembering the old days and the way he'd force a stern look to his face when he had a hand.

Of course, I also assumed I'd get Dorothy before I got any further in my queue.

In fact, I asked the installation guy—a different one, older, but with a similar affect—why I wouldn't have gotten her yet when she'd topped my queue going on three years. He shrugged. I called customer service to complain and the woman on the other end of the line told me she couldn't discuss the particulars of any ghost's queue or how much longer I'd need to wait. When I pressed the issue, the most she'd say was that some ghosts were popular, and it took longer for them to free up.

I asked her about the possibility of terminating my current ghost to get Dorothy early if she were to free up. I was getting my answer—no, I could not—when I turned around to find Maurice smirking at my kitchen table.

He busted out laughing.

Maurice always laughed—the kind of characteristic everyone pointed out, and Maurice had a stock answer: *What else can a black man in America do?* That was the allure of Maurice—a companion who'd laugh easy but also drop a comment now and then to clue you in he was smart and observant—ready to *get into it* with you if you needed him. I remembered getting drunk on gin with him after a card game and opening up about Lucille not being able to have children and him listening, him asking if I really wanted kids, him asking about my marriage, him laughing easy when I made a crack about Lucille's cooking.

There at the kitchen table, Maurice informed me this was his fourth call back to earth. He called his previous residencies *hauntings* and talked about staying with his brother, his widow, and even another of the guys we used to play five-card draw with. We got to talking about married life as a ghost. I teased him, it must have been easier on his side, to be able to dematerialize if he didn't like where the conversation was heading. He laughed and nodded along, but not without pointing out that as the living party, I could leave the apartment altogether and stay gone as long as I wanted.

I suggested we play cards, but in his noncorporeal form we had our limitations. We settled on blackjack, not as much fun without any stakes, without any risk associated with saying *hit me* on seventeen. We whiled away afternoons watching baseball games, and late nights watching war documentaries and John Wayne movies.

Maurice talked about what he missed as a ghost, informing me not being able to taste food was the worst part of being back. He swore he could smell his wife's ribs when he focused hard enough, but even when he leaned into them—tongue outstretched, and concentrated with all his might, he couldn't steal a taste.

Late one night, I talked about Dorothy.

I felt relieved to talk to someone about her. Nobody wants to hear about a dead ex-girlfriend, and least of all my dead wife or dead mother when they were around. Maurice was perfect, though. A sympathetic ear. A fellow man. A captive audience with no better way to spend his time.

He surprised me when he said, "You want to own her."

I didn't like the sound of that. "I guess you could say I want to rent her."

Maurice clicked his tongue and kept his eyes on the TV, even though it showed a commercial for car insurance we'd seen plenty. "If you can rent somebody, it means somebody owns her." He chewed on his thumb. A tick. At first, I read it as almost toddler-like, but I imagined he did it in place of food, wishing, maybe even imagining his thumb were a French fry. "You tell people this Corolla's not my car, I'm leasing it? No, you say this is my car."

I followed him to his natural conclusion. "I don't own you," I said. "I like your company. I thought you liked mine, too."

He laughed. "I like you, Chuck, don't get me wrong." He propped up his feet on the coffee table.

That right there, I thought, *I don't like you having your feet on the table, but I can't stop you, you're your own man.*

"It's not like I can leave anytime I want, though, is it?"

I thought about canceling This Year's Ghost once and for all—I really did. Who needed this kind of grief?

He wouldn't stop laughing, even when I told him to. "People owning people," Maurice said. "I guess we all aren't as evolved as we'd like to think."

#

I decided if I didn't get Dorothy next, I was going to quit. Except then I got Robbie Payton, the singer.

The queues for celebrities were notoriously long, even with premium pricing, and only getting to reserve someone classified as a celebrity once every three years. I'd read speculation This

Year's Ghost even monitored the most requested ghosts to see if they could be reclassified as celebrities, too. Anything to make a buck.

But to have landed Robbie Payton—I'd be a fool to pass up on him.

It's not like I was a die-hard fan, and had I probed the list of celebrity ghosts more thoroughly, I may have found dozens of choices more compelling to me. Still, I was starstruck at the sight of his name and the prospect of having him in my home. I liked his music as a teenager, and Lucille and I had even seen him live on a nostalgia tour a year or two before he passed away. I pictured him singing songs and telling me the stories behind them.

He didn't arrive quietly like the rest, but in a flicker of a light that blew one of the overhead bulbs. Instant *pizzazz*. Sure enough, he was a charmer, gracious when I told him I was a fan. When I called him Mr. Payton, he told me to call him Robbie. Like Maurice, he was at ease with the This Year's Ghost drill. The first night I had him, he watched bootleg video of him on YouTube, and just like I'd imagined it, he told me stories from the road and sang along to a couple of the hits to my applause. We take for granted how well the pros can sing, but even as a ghost, he really did have some pipes on him.

He asked me to turn up the heat a little before I went to bed; odd, because I didn't suppose ghosts could feel the temperature, but I didn't want to question him—he was a guest, wasn't he?

When I woke, Robbie was sitting on the chair by my side, feet propped up on the bed. "You know what I miss?" he said. "The sound of bacon sizzling in a frying pan."

I went out and bought a pack of bacon, just like I went out and bought flowers when he said they'd brighten up the living room and went to replace the flowers I'd picked out with daisies after he clarified those were the kinds of flowers he'd meant. We listened to his music again the next night, and the night after, and the night after.

It would've been nice to hear Dorothy sing if I ever got her ghost.

I mentioned something to Robbie about how he must be getting sick of hearing his songs over and over again, and I didn't mind if we watched a movie instead, but he brushed me off, drilling into the details of what a pain it was to work with the producer for his third album. "No ear," Robbie said. "He thought music was a formula—plug in verses and a chorus and a bridge and move on to the next one. No *soul*."

A week in, Robbie asked me to move one of the This Year's Ghost containment devices out onto the balcony. "I want to feel the sun again. That's probably the worst part of this ghost gig, you know, chief? Being cooped up inside all the time."

He always called me *chief* or *boss* or *my friend*. It felt intimate at first. After a month or so, I put together he'd forgotten my name.

Still, I wanted to be a good host, so I set to moving the device—a trickier proposition than it seemed at first glance. I don't have much head for electronics, and I'd never put much thought into these things since Bud installed them. They seemed important, though, emitting a light buzzing sound, plugged into the walls with short power cords, somehow or other connected, too, to a backup generator in case we lost power.

"Unplug the thing, boss. We'll plug it in again as soon as you have it in position. Ten seconds, what's it going to matter?" Robbie's voice took on a bit of an edge, like he was losing his patience with me.

Five seconds passed, and my phone rang. A woman from This Year's Ghost spoke from the other end of the line.

"We're showing a disconnected container at your residence. Are you home, sir?"

I marveled at how quickly they'd called—how seriously the company must take this sort of thing. Most of all, I got that flushed feeling in my face, like when I was in school and somebody talked me into letting them copy off my paper, or I joined the pack in pushing around some nerd right before a teacher arrived on the scene. *I'm not the one who should be in trouble, honest!* my younger self opined.

"I was just moving it a little," I said.

"You must leave that to the professionals, sir. We can schedule a service appointment, but for now your terms of service require you leave the container where the technician installed it."

I knew well enough that *terms of service* meant contract law and big fines or termination of my subscription. Termination didn't sound so awful then, but I didn't like the feeling of getting into hot water, so while I was still on the phone, and over Robbie's complaints I was *a goddamn boy scout* I plugged it back in.

#

I kept on with This Year's Ghost. Got a high school friend next, who was at least less grating than Robbie turned out to be. Then a girl from my old office I used to flirt with who was, at least, still flirty, though without the sense of danger we might do something with one another, the whole thing rang hollow. She was still pretty, sure, but that only underscored how much I wanted to see Dorothy again. I had this memory of how she looked standing by my bedroom window, peeking between the blinds to check the weather in the morning. I wanted to see her like that again, even if she were more silhouette and shadow, more ghost than girl.

I called This Year's Ghost again to complain about still waiting on Dorothy. I asked if this was how they scammed their customers—keep them hanging on the hopes they'll see their first choice. I got the same, mechanical response about it being a longer wait for some ghosts than others, and no, she couldn't disclose how much longer I'd have to wait.

I wasn't getting any younger. I didn't have people over often, and when they did come, the ghost became something to explain—why I'd picked that one, or, to the real oblivious, old-timer luddites, what This Year's Ghost was in the first place. By the end of the visit, we'd obligatorily joke when one of us was gone maybe the other would host their ghost. It might have made me a hypocrite, but I wasn't sure I liked the idea of having to move into one of their homes. Where would I sleep? Or would I sleep at all? How much longer would a day, a week, a year *feel* without sleeping?

I'd given up hope and renewed my annual resolve to cancel This Year's Ghost when Dorothy, at last, arrived.

#

Dorothy came to me young. She'd died young, late forties or early fifties if my memory from the newspaper obituary served. She'd moved out of town decades ago, made a go of it in New York, and even starred in a play off-Broadway, the story said.

She looked younger than forty in my apartment—maybe it was on account of my old eyes. She wore the blue dress I'd recognize anywhere. The one she wore on stage for *A Christmas Carol.*

Dorothy was polite. She told me it was good to see me and I had a beautiful home and asked all the courtesy questions about my wife and if I'd had kids that you're supposed to ask after you haven't seen someone for a matter of decades. I asked her about her time as a ghost. I tried hard not to spill all the beans about how she'd been my first choice from the get-go.

You couldn't accuse Dorothy of talking too much, that's for sure. Of her previous hosts, *they were fine,* and if the fluorescent light fixture were bothering, *it's all right, thanks.* All the while, she sat on the opposite end of the couch, legs crossed tight, compact as she could be.

I opened a bottle of Chardonnay. Social lubricant. Sure, she couldn't drink, but I figured if I were looser lipped, it'd get her started, too.

No dice.

Instead, I wound up telling her I was paying for her to be there, so couldn't she say *something*?

She said she was sorry, but in a way that made me sorry because it was the mumbled apology of a scolded child or a beaten wife. No apology at all, but an admission of defeat.

I told her she could have the guest room. I'd close the door and wouldn't bother her until she wanted to see me. If she wanted the TV or some music for her, all she had to do was ask.

The next day, I weighed what it would mean to smash the containers, too. What was the worst This Year's Ghost could do? Ban me for life? Sue me for what little I was worth?

I'd thought of it after I'd closed the door, though. I didn't want to do anything drastic without asking her first, and I didn't want to go back on my word about leaving her alone as long as she wanted.

A week went by.

I watched the door for signs of movement and kept an eye on the way light shone through the edges between the door and doorframe in mid-morning. The room looked much darker, at least from those edges, in the afternoon. I'd never noticed before.

Then I heard her.

She sang.

She sang a song about a bluebird flying, and I remembered, more so than those nights of community theater, when I caught her singing to herself in the early morning one time—maybe the same morning she'd peeked between the blinds, but it all runs together after enough years—making eggs for the both of us in my kitchen. She sounded the way warm apple pie smells coming out of the oven Thanksgiving morning. Like sweetness. Like home. I didn't say a word. I listened, and I waited for her to turn around and see me.

Dog Days

From back before all the dogs were gone, I remember Waffles. The first time Waffles stole a waffle from Dad's plate (the reason we renamed him from Rover). Waffles barking from the far side of the front door when I keyed into the house. The way Waffles smelled when he was wet—moist and mildew-y in a way that made it seem as though he'd never be dry again. That look on his face when he was happy. People say dogs couldn't smile, but I swear Waffles did every day I knew him.

Then Waffles got sick. He was slower one day and sneezy. Other dogs got sick, too. So many it made the news.

Waffles' fur started to fall off.

He'd shiver and whimper and I tried to hold him close, but Mom said it wasn't a good idea. She said I shouldn't touch Waffles.

I went to school. I came home. No barks from the far side of the door or scraping of his nails against the wood. No thump of his tail against the floor. Mom opened the door before I could get it unlocked all the way. Already home. She told me they'd put Waffles to sleep.

I hated her. Couldn't understand at the time it was better to let some things die than to draw out suffering. I understand now, even though I still resent not getting to say goodbye.

But that's how dogs went. Not just Waffles, but whole breeds, and then the entire species, gone inside of a year. Plenty of theories made the rounds, but no could give any real reason why.

The world split. On one side stood the dog lovers. Those who had had dogs or wished they'd had dogs, and in either case felt a profound loss at having nothing but photographs and videos to commemorate their existence. On the other side of the line stood people who didn't much seem to care, or who even seemed pleased at not having to worry about stepping in poop on the sidewalk.

There's a way in which such divisions were good. Useful. I could see immediately the dog haters weren't worth knowing.

And then I met Holly.

Holly wasn't like the rest of the people who hadn't known dogs. She was curious. And she listened. Maybe it's just because the two of us went from sitting next to each other in US History to flirting to having phone calls that kept us up past one on school nights. Maybe she loved me enough to love hearing about dogs. But I could see a difference. You didn't have to have had a dog to be a dog person. To have a good heart. To be loyal. To be up for a waffle at any time of day or night

It broke my heart that she never knew a dog's love. But it broke my heart even more that after we'd graduated and after we'd married, our little girl Spirit would never encounter a dog at all. To her, dogs were like dinosaurs—some relic from a time past that only seemed vaguely possible, but never a part of day-to-day life. For all I know, she may have seen the old photographs of me with Waffles and might as well have been looking at me posed with a unicorn for how strange and unbelievable such a creature looked.

We got her a cat, at my insistence it was good for a child to care for an animal, and after Holly got won over by Poof—named for his thick plume of white fur that made it look like he was in a constant state of electric shock. I never fell in love with the cat the way I'd fallen in love with Waffles. I'm not sure it's possible for a man to love a cat the way he loves a dog. Poof nonetheless became a part of the family—as a good substitute as we could find for the kind of animal companion I might have hoped for.

When Holly decided we had married too young and weren't really a good fit for one another, she got Spirit five days out of the week; I got Poof seven for seven. I didn't particularly want the fur ball and might have let Holly have him or given him to a shelter were it not for the fact I could see Spirit had formed her own connection with him. Then it became a matter of pride, and a matter of shoring up my daughter's affections, that she would associate Poof with Dad. Even if she wanted to stay in her normal bed and play with all the toys she was used to after a long week of school, she would want to come to Dad's Friday night if for no other reason to chase down Poof and touch noses and give him a squeeze.

And so we lived this pattern. During the week, Poof alternated between stretches of aloof solitude when he hid in a suitcase or a kitchen cupboard and starving for attention and stretching himself across my laptop keyboard or leaping onto the kitchen table to stare me down from an inch's distance as I ate SpaghettiOs or Ramen.

And then the dog arrived.

I was at my computer, studying Holly's Facebook photos. She hadn't posted a new one for a month, but I scrolled as if I'd find one that had previously escaped my attention. I wish I could say it was the only time. I paused on a picture of her in a two-piece bathing suit. In our years together—our years of marriage—I don't recall ever having seen her in a two-piece, too body conscious and modest. But there she was at sunset, hands on her hips, back to the camera, mid-step at a hotel pool. No one else around. The photo first surfaced in the middle of the week in winter, so the upload couldn't have synched up with when it happened. And she'd uploaded it herself. All of a sudden proud of this moment, this photograph, posted to an album called *Adventuring* which otherwise featured images of her picking blueberries with Spirit, posing over a plate of fresh-baked chocolate chip cookies, puzzling over a chessboard. It was the first photo of hers to make me wonder who was behind the camera. Who she had her head cocked toward, neck turned as if she were in the process of noticing to the photographer, though she didn't appear annoyed (strange because she didn't like candid photographs).

I hadn't managed to shake the question since.

Like I said—then the dog arrived.

I had a ground-level apartment, and birds and squirrels trespassed all the time. Poof originally chased them away from the opposite side of the glass, but had grown into watching more calmly, from a distance so the smaller animals wouldn't see him. From that range, Poof silently moved his mouth in a chewing motion.

Poof noticed the dog before me. Was already taking stutter-steps toward the glass door, the way he'd sometimes approach his reflection in the full-length mirror in my bedroom. That fundamental knowledge that something about what he was seeing was not right. That instinctive fear of the unknown.

The dog staggered. Not favoring any particular leg but walking as if he were wounded, as if he'd already walked a hundred miles. A sheepdog—didn't they always look sort of pathetic? He had white and gray fur like bangs all but covering his eyes, and his jaw wiggled as if he were trying to muster a bark.

Poof hissed.

I stood beside him. I didn't want to scare the dog away. A real, live dog! Gently, but firmly, I ushered Poof aside with my shin the way I would when he got in the way while I had a pot on the stove or when I was trying to comb my hair, late for work. I ushered him aside visibly, as if to show this dog that of the two creatures who lived in this apartment, the larger one welcomed him. I opened the door.

#

I named the new dog Waffles. He wasn't so much like the old Waffles, but a rather a generally exhausted, floppy dog who didn't demonstrate much interest in the waffle I, naturally, tried to feed him. Instead, he fixated on licking a spot on the floor.

Waffles barked when the doorbell rang. I should have expected it. Since I'd washed him off in the tub, trimmed the fur from his eyes, and fed him half a steak, he'd revitalized and started barking in response to Poof when he hissed, barking when gunshots were fired on TV, barking when the microwave beeped to announce another meal was ready.

I should have predicted he'd bark at the doorbell and should have headed it off when Holly came by with Spirit Friday afternoon. Waffles got all excited and Poof, who'd napped on the couch, sprinted off to the bedroom or bathroom like he did at each reminder Waffles existed. Holly and Spirit were, predictably, taken aback.

Spirit had never heard a dog bark in real life before.

I could see through the front window they'd taken a step back from the house, and I hurried to open the door.

Waffles ran up to them and barked—not a mean bark, but a loud one, and he pursued Spirit with his nose as she backed away from him.

Holly backed up too and angled her body as if to get between Spirit and Waffles. "Chuck, what's going on?"

I told her about Waffles' arrival—not that I was looking at pictures of her when I first encountered him, of course, but that he'd walked up to the door. No tags because who owned a dog these days? What dogs were there? But wasn't it incredible? And Waffles was friendly and well-behaved aside from the barking. He'd even waited to go outside to do his business, and I'd fashioned a leash using an old belt for a collar, duct-taped to a tape measure that would expand and retract as we walked. He didn't show much interest in running. He seemed old. Maybe a survivor, somehow, from the old days. A secret pup who'd made it in the wild, or, more likely, with some other master.

Holly asked Spirit to wait in the car. "Your father and I need to talk."

"She can come inside," I said.

"The dog should go inside."

Inside, I understood, was a mutually exclusive space for Spirit and Waffles, but in that moment, Spirit seemed to warm to the mutt. She scratched behind his ears, not unlike the way she would with Poof, who often as not squirmed and ran. Waffles leaned into it. Wagged his tail, strong and wide. Joyful.

"Please," Holly repeated, an edge to her voice.

Spirit listened, slowly walking back to the car. I bent over and put a hand to Waffles' side to keep him from following after her, though his eyes stuck on her in a stare I could only assume Holly would describe as creepy. I snapped my fingers behind him, and he turned around, obedient, if sullen, and went inside far enough for me to pull the door shut behind him.

"Is it a good idea to have some strange animal around our daughter?"

"For Christ's sake, he's a dog, not a rhinoceros. Poof would probably hurt her before Waffles would."

"It barked at her."

"He didn't know her. And didn't you see how quickly he let her pet him? And she liked him, too."

Holly sighed. "No one's seen a dog since we were kids and then this one shows up at your door. Don't you think that's suspicious?"

I liked it when she got angry. A dirty little secret, but the volume and the tone of her voice when she got agitated was close to how she sounded mid-coitus. Not just that, but the way her nose wrinkled in indignation and in ecstasy—also very similar. I only noticed these things after she'd told me we were through and savored them in the aftermath. Often as not, I preferred it when we fought to when she was acting nicely toward me. The latter was an act, but the former was real and intense, and her flesh would turn pink for forcing out too many words, not taking in enough air.

"He's a well-behaved dog. Nothing's gone wrong since he got here, besides Poof getting spooked."

Spirit was in the front passenger seat of Holly's car, up on her knees, so her head almost hit the ceiling, leaning over the console, over the dash, peering forward, smiling with her mouth wide open. I followed her line of sight back to the house. Waffles was on the couch, front paws up on the back of it, mouth open wide, unmistakably smiling back.

"Promise me, Chuck." Holly had her hands on her hips, not unlike the photograph by the pool, her body pointed toward me, head cocked back toward Spirit. "Promise me the second that thing does anything dangerous, or the second Spirit says she's scared, you'll get rid of it."

She trusted me just enough to care for our daughter under the rules we'd come up with together when we were parenting in the same place, at the same time. Not enough to improvise.

"I promise."

#

The worst thing to happen during Spirit's first visit with Waffles around was that, when Poof fled her arms because he saw Waffles coming, he scratched her skin in his hurry to escape. Waffles fell at her feet and exposed his belly, and Spirit was immediately distracted from the white line Poof had left on her forearm, in favor of giving Waffles a rub and laughing with glee as he thumped his tail mightily against the floor.

I took photographs of Spirit and Waffles. Waffles returning the tennis ball she'd thrown for him in the backyard. Spirit hugging Waffles from behind before she went to bed. I sent them one by one to Holly. She still called Friday night, three times Saturday, and once Sunday before she came to pick up Spirit after dinner. The subtext was clear: she expected me not to answer, because Waffles had taken a turn and attacked us both. Holly did soften a bit each time, though, and when she came to the apartment, she even went so far as to pat Waffles on the head and laughed rather than recoiled when he got up on his back paws to hug his body against her.

Poof watched from atop the kitchen cabinets, full of scorn.

But Poof was a relic from a dogless past life we'd all partaken in, in which Holly had left me. In this new life, we had Waffles, and the following week Spirit brought along a squeaky baby toy for him to play with. She explained, *Mom told me dogs used to like toys like this*. In this life, things were getting better. In this life,

Holly posted a new photograph to Facebook. One for which she was neither photographer nor subject, but rather recipient—a selfie *I* had sent her of Waffles, Spirit, and I all curled up on the sofa together, the three of us all looking so happy. It got likes. It got comments. From what I could gather, everyone assumed we'd Photoshopped it somehow, inserting this long-extinct dog in between us.

I didn't Photoshop anything. But I did open a separate window so I could look at the picture of Holly in the bathing suit and this new photo in juxtaposition to one another, shifted and resized until I could imagine we were all in the same picture together. Happy together. A family.

And then Holly texted me, Wednesday night at 10:08, eight minutes after Spirit would have gone to bed. She texted me, *what do you say we go for a walk tomorrow night?*

Holly left Spirit with her mom. I left Waffles and Poof home alone. Not like I didn't do that every day when I went to work, but it was unusual for me to be out at night. Poof was hiding when I left, but Waffles followed me all the way to the door, as if I were taking him on this moonlight stroll, and he whimpered when I closed the door behind me without him.

I was outside early. A change of pace because I habitually ran late—one of my many shortcomings Holly cited when she left me, one of the reasons she always picked up and dropped off Spirit, so I'd never leave her waiting.

She wore a long-sleeved, flowing black shirt, blue jeans, and black boots. Not the clothes she would have worn at work. Not entirely casual, but not exactly dressed up either. I didn't recognize the shirt. She smelled incredible, like dandelions and citrus.

I got too excited, I know, but once we started walking, I couldn't help myself from talking about summer and having friends watch Poof while the four of us—me, Holly, Spirit, and

Waffles—went somewhere new and exotic, where we could spend some time at a pool and Waffles could run around to his heart's content, and maybe he'd want to doggie paddle in the water, too.

When Holly took my hand, I was ready. Nervous, sure, but ready to be the husband I should've been all along. I'd dress better and start jogging to stave off my paunch and we'd stop rock-paper-scissoring over dish-washing duty. I'd just do it.

"I met somebody else," she said.

As we walked by, a set of sprinklers turned on. The water reached far enough to hit my tennis shoes as I walked past, closest to the lawn They were probably on a timer, and we probably had bad luck, passing by when we did, but I didn't put it past whoever lived inside to have turned on the water more purposefully to keep us moving.

"Things have moved quickly." She loosened her grip for a second and pulled away, then gave my fingers a squeeze. "He asked me to marry him."

I squinted at the house, studying the blinds in the front window for movement, or to see if anyone's fingers were parting them, and if I might catch their eyes watching us. I'd glare back at them. Maybe give them a crazed yell.

"Chuck, I'm moving to Philadelphia. With Spirit."

I would have questions. *Could* she legally move out of state under our joint custody agreement? Who on earth was this boyfriend of hers? How quick was *quickly*? When did they intend to move? Had they had sex, and was that what Holly did all the weekends when I had Spirit? Had this other man taken the photograph of her in the two-piece? Had she chosen now to let me down because I had Waffles to keep me company? All of those questions would wait until after the whimper I could neither suppress, nor cut off in time to come across as a sane human being. That whimper cost me whatever remained of a last chance of convincing her, *no*, she and I belonged together.

#

Waffles slowed down. One night, he lay down, curled on the floor beside the couch and wagged his tail with a slow, irregular rhythm. Slower, slower, until it stopped.

I like to think the fact he was wagging in the end meant he died happy.

I called Holly and explained what had happened. I said Spirit should be there. My best guess is she felt this was a small favor to pay, so she didn't put up a fight, even though it was the middle of the week.

I'd dug a hole in the backyard already. We loaded Waffles on a blanket. Holly and Spirit each took an adjacent corner, and I took the opposite side to lift Waffles, to lower him. I shoveled the dirt over him and Spirit hummed "Amazing Grace."

As I shoveled, it occurred to me all the phrases that used dog in a pejorative sense, like *dog days* and *he's dogging it* and *it's a dog-eat-dog world* had fallen out of vernacular. Maybe it had to do with remembering our canine friends fondly, but equally likely it was a matter of obscurity. Dogs were gone so why speak of them?

The hole in the yard full, Waffles at rest, Holly hugged me. Of the three of us, she was the only one to cry in the moment. Spirit yawned. It was past her bedtime.

It was too late at night to eat without tempting indigestion, but after Holly and Spirt left, I put two waffles in the toaster. I poured myself a glass of milk and fetched the plastic bottle of maple syrup from the fridge door. The kitchen started to smell of burning, and by the time I got back to the toaster, the coils were hot orange, the edges of my snack crispy, black, and wasted.

Stone

I was in the eighth grade when Duncan, the boy made of stone, moved in next door. Word got around he'd gotten in big trouble at his old school and that's how his family wound up in Lakeville. But unlike the kids whose reputations as brawlers or shoplifters made them cool, Duncan wasn't the beneficiary of any dangerous chic. We hung out—first out of the happenstance of living so close by, then out of habit—but despite his insistence, I never wanted to call him my friend.

Why wasn't Duncan cool? For one thing, he talked *so* slowly, elongating every vowel sound to a painful extreme. Small talk was excruciating and even the teachers stopped calling on him because he took three or four times as long as anybody else in class to get an idea across.

Another mark against Duncan: the kid was terrified of water, and particularly the lake in the middle of town. "Do you blame me?" he asked. "Imagine if you were made of two hundred-fifty pounds of rock. There's no floating for me." The thing is, everyone loved the lake. For tanning, for swimming, for kayaking. It's where all of the high schoolers hung out in the warmer months, and on that outer edge of middle school, it's where eighth graders with aspirations of cool wanted to be, too.

Strike three: Becky Fieldings, the nicest girl in school from the wealthiest family in town, invited him to her thirteenth birthday party in September. Everyone was pretty annoyed with the way he talked. Some of the guys started poking fun at how he nervously rocked when he got anywhere near the swimming pool after the party moved out back. but what really sealed the deal was when Duncan petted Becky's cocker spaniel too hard— an accident, but he *broke the dog's back*. Mr. Fieldings yelled at him and called him a criminal and Duncan shuffled off as fast as he could (which wasn't fast), chin tucked into his chest, shoulders caved in.

On top of all that, there was the matter of baseball. When you're in the eighth grade, there are few things less cool than the inability to swing a bat and make contact with the ball in gym class, at recess, in pickup games at the park. It didn't help that Duncan couldn't run fast enough to field any play, but his swing was *brutally* slow. His only saving grace was his command of gravity. Every now and again, he could get his arms to drop at the right time, and slam the bat down on the ball, and make it ricochet off the ground into his version of a pop fly.

I wasn't so good at hitting the ball myself—below average in hand-eye coordination, with little enough upper body strength that for every at-bat, the opposing team huddled in closer, certain my mightiest hit wouldn't reach past the pitcher's mound. My lone advantage in baseball—not to mention soccer, basketball, volleyball, and escaping a pounding from the rough kids at school—was I could run like hell. It's the sort of ability that makes you a smidge more socially acceptable, but perhaps more importantly let me run my way out of trouble, escaping noogies and swirlies.

In the years leading up to the eighth grade, I don't know that I would have rejected Duncan's friendship. But this was the eighth grade, and I was deeply, profoundly in love with Anastasia, the girl made of glass.

Anastasia. Thin and delicate. My first imaginings of the female form climaxed in what it might look like to see straight through her sweater, her camisole, to her veins and to her heart. Her voice just shy of shrill, and she spoke up in class all of the time, not in a know-it-all kind of way, but as though she were really interested in *Huckleberry Finn* and the quadratic equation and geopolitical implications, until it made me wonder if I ought to be interested, too. All of a sudden lectures and readings and essays weren't only work, but an opportunity to share headspace with Anastasia.

In April, the Spring Swing loomed. An annual dance for eighth graders, leading into the summer before high school. We talked about it then in similar ways to how we would talk about prom four years later. We weren't after sex, but our first trips to first base and the prayer of stealing second. I harbored dreams of leaving the dance with Anastasia for a girlfriend.

"Nobody asks Annie," Howard said. He'd summoned us eighth grade boys into a huddle in the locker room before gym class. No one could corral people around him quite like Howard, the boy made of fire, who'd moved past self-consciousness about his flaming body in the first grade and assumed the role of prankster and bully, inflicting first degree burns if you wouldn't let him copy off of your math quiz (and sometimes simply for his own amusement). The edges of him would flicker in a white hot, smoky haze.

Howard called Anastasia Annie. She told him she didn't like it, but he seemed to take it as banter rather than a meaningful complaint. "I'm taking her to the dance. You got a problem with that, Jordan?"

"No problem." I didn't know why he singled me out. If anything, I'd aimed to harden my face to not to show any concern, as though I'd never planned on going to the dance at all, let alone on asking Anastasia.

"Good." Howard stood up straight and the boys behind him backed away. He had grown taller and broader than the rest of us, bigger by every dimension. Bigger, so we weren't certain he understood the size of his own flames.

#

I skipped stones over the water, at a shallow part of the lake by my house where hardly anyone ever went. The skipping was a habit from before Duncan moved to town, but I'd be lying if I said I didn't take small pleasure in watching him wince as the stones bounce-bounce-bounced and finally sank. He never asked me to stop, but kept a safe distance from the water himself, sitting a couple feet behind me when I stepped to the water's edge.

"Howard's a flaming turd," Duncan said. "If she goes to the dance, she should go with you."

This was another dimension of Duncan's lack of cool. He said motherly things. I could tell he was getting more comfortable around me, though, because now and again he'd let the sweet exterior drop. Like when he was first figuring out my crush on Anastasia after he caught me staring at her at school, and asked, *do you get more like me around her?* and I asked what he meant, and he knocked against his stone head. *You know, hard.* I kicked his shin, but it only hurt my foot, and he laughed.

"Maybe she'll say no to Howard." I sat down beside him in the grass. "Then I can ask."

Duncan shook his head slowly. "She's too nice."

We both knew it was true. Anastasia, who never rolled her eyes when teachers asked her to transcribe notes on the board. Anastasia, who wrote a personal thank you note for every cardboard valentine she got in elementary school. Anastasia who rotated lunch tables to sit with every different group of girls. She wasn't capable of saying no. The first person to ask would get to hold her hand, get to whisper in her ear, get that first slow dance.

"You have to ask her."

The sun beat down at a sharp angle, too hot for this early in the spring. It reflected right off the water into our eyes, so it seemed to hit us from two different angles. "Howard would fry me if he saw me get close to her."

"Let me take care of that."

#

We formed a plan. Maybe Duncan considered it a test: help me get the girl, and I couldn't deny him as a friend—as my best friend—ever again, not to mention he'd promised to have my back if Howard came after me. "You can't burn stone. But you can stomp out a flame."

The scheme was simple. Anastasia went to Science Club after school every Wednesday. This week, I'd go too and as soon as the opportunity presented itself—Duncan was adamant about that part, after a lifetime of being too slow—I'd ask her if she would go to the dance with me. In the meantime, Duncan would distract Howard. He and his friends usually played football after school, and Duncan would interject himself after the game, talking football, talking school, talking girls, even subjecting himself to abuse if he needed to keep Howard from coming to the science labs. Howard would be angry afterward, for sure, and might burn me or get some of his cronies to pummel me. But once Anastasia had agreed to go to the dance with me, he'd have to turn his attentions elsewhere—to finding his own date, or to making up his mind the dance was stupid, and he didn't want to go in the first place.

Life would progress in new trajectories. Anastasia my girl. Duncan my friend.

I'd gone to Science Club a couple times before. When they were dissecting frogs because I wanted to see what the amphibious innards might look like, and when they built baking soda volcanos. The day I was going to ask Anastasia to the dance, spindly old Mr. Pawelec, compulsively clad in a stained white lab coat, stood in front of the lab and explained it was Day One of Two working on egg drops. A buffet of materials awaited us— packing peanuts, paper towel rolls, scotch tape, aluminum foil, balloons. We would have all period to work in pairs to build our contraptions and then experiment with dropping our eggs from increasingly great heights the following meeting.

He released us to find our partners. I had maneuvered my way to standing right beside Anastasia but didn't want to look over-eager. I wanted to be casual. Cool. But then Chester—a chubby boy with browned fingertips who smelled like blueberries tapped my shoulder and asked if we could work together. I faced Anastasia, just as she and Whitney Brooks agreed to partner up.

We worked on our egg drop, or rather Chester did. I was more invested in stealing snippets of what Anastasia had to say about fragility and safe packing, touching each piece of their own construction materials with glass fingertips.

When the after-school period was over, when I saw my opportunity slipping away, Anastasia came within arm's reach. I called her name.

I stalled, waiting for more people to file out, waiting for Mr. Pawelec to be too tied up in a student question to eavesdrop. She waited with me but avoided eye contact while I fidgeted with a rubber band left over from Chester's handiwork.

Finally, Anastasia and I were alone.

Once I got going, the words tumbled out, simple and at least clear. "I want to go to the Spring Swing with you—what do you think?"

"That's really nice, Jordan," she said. "And I'd like to. But Howard asked at lunchtime. But maybe we can have a dance together? Assuming Howard doesn't mind."

My blood boiled. It was almost worse that she was nice. The confirmation that had I asked yesterday, I'd be going with her.

The only real solace I could take from the moment was if Howard had already asked, then he'd never have to know I'd defied him. And maybe Duncan—trying to slow him down, trying to keep him occupied—had made his afternoon a little worse. I could see Duncan and I skipping the dance and sitting by the lake that night. But no, I didn't want to torture him with water anymore after he had tried to help, so maybe I'd even invite him over to the house. I didn't trust him not to break my Nintendo 64 controllers, but maybe we could eat pizza and watch TV.

I pictured all of this while Anastasia walked out of the room, her footsteps light as a child's, so little to weigh her down until they stopped when she reached the hall. "Oh, hi Howard."

Against all logic, against the glint of fire that reflected off the classroom windows and against the warmer air approaching from behind me, I was chilled.

Howard said something to her about how he forgot a notebook in the lab earlier today and how he was so excited to take her to the dance and about how he hoped she had a good afternoon. Then Anastasia was gone. And he was there.

He was there with Kevin Riley and Jamie Fowlkes, a pair of big, strong kids who were menaces in gym class dodgeball games and had engineered the biggest, soggiest spitballs known to man, settling not for the cafeteria straws, but bubble tea straws they got outside the school. Wider. More powerful.

Riley and Fowlkes each grabbed one of my upper arms and pinned my back to lab table, bent me over backward slightly so when Howard got in my face, he had to curve his body to match mine, and I hardly trusted him to do so with care.

"I want to go to the dance with you. What do you think?" He repeated my words with a moron's inflection, low and slow, not unlike Duncan when he got nervous and, rather than sputtering, worked himself up to almost the tempo of ordinary speech. "You don't even know how to talk to a girl."

"You're right." Sweat welled up in my armpits and over my forehead. Having Howard so close was like standing next to a furnace. I tried to concoct excuses. Along the lines that I was asking her and asking her so poorly on purpose so Howard would look better by comparison. Not that Anastasia ever would have turned him down, of course, but to make the choice even clearer. To make her fall in love with him—strong, better spoken, clearly better than me.

"You're lucky I already asked Annie to the dance." Even his eyes were fire, his pupils a smidge darker than the rest of him. I wondered if he saw the world through a flickering orange filter. "You didn't know I'd asked, did you?"

Mr. Pawelec would come back. He had to. With Mr. Pawelec watching, he'd have to let me go.

Howard might have smiled. Impossible to tell when he was up close and looked more like a campfire. The best I could do was to read shapes in the whims of flames.

"Maybe I oughta burn you, so you don't keep making eyes at my girl." He edged two fingers to within an inch of my eyes. If someone blew a fan behind him, my corneas would've been toast.

I cried. What else could I do? Take away Riley and Fowlkes and I don't know if I would have trusted myself to run, even. He'd have caught up to me. This boy who brought his own aluminum bat for gym class, because he couldn't hold the wooden one without engulfing it. This boy who always made contact and whose blur was almost beautiful as he streaked from home plate to first base and onward. I did my best to keep my body from convulsing but didn't bother to stop myself from crying. Tears rolled into sweat until my face was soaked.

"You're pathetic, Jordan. A real pussy." Howard backed away.

"Yeah, pussy," Fowlkes echoed.

The guys let me go, and I crumpled to the floor.

Duncan was nowhere to be found.

#

I missed the late bus, so I had to walk back. I wasn't in the mood to go home, though, so I took a winding route to a different part of the lake and ambled along the perimeter toward my neighborhood. I imagined somehow luring Howard to the water's edge and then shoving him in so I could watch him flail in the water. I couldn't imagine helping him. And in that moment, he'd know what it felt like to be helpless.

Alternately, I imagined seeing Anastasia in the water. In my fantasy, she was drowning, and I saved her, and her whole body was trembling and so slippery as I ferried her to safety, as I cradled her close to warm her.

The sun was starting to set by the time I neared home. I was probably late for dinner and faced the damning situation of not wanting to listen to my mother scold me and knowing she'd scold me worse for every minute longer I stayed outside.

Before I could get home, I came upon Duncan. It was strange to see him at the water, and I wondered if he'd sensed I would come there to skip rocks and shout curse words.

There's this feeling you get sometimes. When you're too mad to forgive someone, even though you know you probably ought to. When you're equal parts mad at them and mad at yourself because you put yourself in a position to be mad over something that can't be helped. I registered all of this. I figured I'd walk straight past him, *maybe* tell him to give me some goddamned space, but that would be the end of it.

"I'm so sorry," he said.

Hearing his slow, stupid voice, all I could do was hate him. I eyed his position, a few feet from the water. I'd seen him lose his balance sometimes and roll. He had hard time picking himself up, and a hard time stopping his body once it had gathered momentum.

"I tried to keep him there," Duncan said, "but when I asked about the dance, he knew something was up."

I pushed him, scraping the palm of my hand against his surface.

"I'm sorry."

"You're a real piece of shit." I curled my fingers into fist, imagining them something like balls of stone. Imagining hurting him. "This is why no one likes you. You're worthless."

"Please."

"*Please.*" I managed the stretch *e* sound even longer than he had, so he could hear how ridiculous he was. I spat on him in the process. Then I punched his chin, and my fingers felt like they exploded on impact. He took a step back, tilted his head. He had felt it at least, even if he didn't fall or cry out. Even if my knuckles gushed blood. "What are you going to do? Cry? You're pathetic. You're a pussy."

He pushed me down. I'd never expected it, somehow. Maybe I'd never thought of him as so different from a stone I'd kick down the street, or one I'd skip over the surface of the lake— inconsequential and subject to my whims, never the other way around. I'd never seen him move so fast as he did when he fell on top of me, smashing my rib cage beneath his weight.

I angled my head to look to the water. If I could inch our bodies that way, it might spook Duncan, and he'd retreat for fear of falling in. The surface of the water was perfectly smooth and still.

When I looked back, Duncan had cocked back his fist to punch me. My last thought was that I was going to die, and, at the end of the worst day of my life, I hardly cared.

#

Duncan didn't kill me. I don't know if I'll ever fully understand why. Maybe he remembered I was his friend. Maybe he remembered the particulars of whatever happened in his last school, his last town. Whatever the reason, he mustered more restraint than I had that evening, stopping himself before he did something he couldn't take back.

Someone found me at the side of the lake and called an ambulance. It's possible Duncan had gotten away on foot—I'm fuzzy on the timeline—but it's more likely he waited in the thick of trees, standing stock still so no one would ever notice him watching over me.

I told the police I didn't remember what had happened. They assumed I got mugged, which didn't make a ton of sense given my knapsack and my wallet were still intact, but they made up the excuse someone came along and scared the criminals away. For a few weeks, parents were more nervous than usual about letting their kids walk home from school or hang out with friends after dusk. Like everything, that, too, would fade, and by summer life in Lakeville went back to normal.

I was banged up. A bad concussion and three broken ribs. I sat out the rest of the school year and took makeup exams at the end of the summer so I could still move on to high school.

I caught glimpses of Duncan a few times from my bedroom window, walking down the street. Maybe he meant for me to call out to him and invite him inside. I almost did once.

Duncan's family moved away over the summer. I haven't seen him since.

Howard left me alone the next school year. I guess he'd tortured me enough that I could confirm he was dangerous to anyone who asked. In the fall, I was happy to see no sign of him and Anastasia dating. Then some seniors pulled a prank—they went at Howard with a fire extinguisher. He lashed out and burned a couple of the guys pretty badly, plus one of the teachers who tried to split up the brawl. Everyone got suspended, but Howard never came back. Rumor had it the school told his family Lakeville High wasn't a good fit for him.

I never talked much with Anastasia—not anything more than hellos and how are yous and the one time Mr. Barkley paired us in US History, junior year. She'd had a car accident the summer before and broke her arm—the kind of injury that would heal for most people, but everything between her right shoulder and her elbow had shattered. She had been right-handed, so I, like all her partners, did all the writing for our assignment and tried not to stare.

I was a senior when a girl named Stella transferred into Lakeville High, a sophomore who had previously lived in the city. Only the second person made of stone I'd ever seen. She smoked cigarettes and cursed a lot, and talked slowly, but had developed enough of a rhythm in her speech that she didn't elongate words the way Duncan had. She had adapted. Normalized. Blended in.

We started dating in the late fall. I bought her a fourteen-karat gold necklace with a phony diamond pendant for Christmas and she wore it faithfully for the months to follow, stone bouncing against stone at her chest. I borrowed my father's car to take her to prom.

After the dance, we went to a party on the opposite side of the lake from where I lived. The guys from the football team brought a keg. By the end of the night, folks skinny dipped. The other boys' bodies underscored how scrawny I was with their broader frames and athletes' muscle. And the girls. I knew I shouldn't stare after they'd let me into this inner circle, but how could a boy resist taking mental photographs of hips and wet hair clinging to bare shoulders?

I turned to Stella. I had held off on hanging out at the lake with her, never wanting to force her into the same slow psychological torture I'd subjected Duncan to. I understood the fear of water now. The practicalities of sinking, of getting in over your head. The thin line between breathing and feeling like your insides were on fire. The difference between control and feeling helpless, and how quickly a person could transition between the two. I told her I could take her home if she wanted.

She shook her head. "We should stay." She pulled the straps of her dress down from her shoulders and then asked for my help to unzip her back. I stripped clumsily in front of her, embarrassed at how slight I was and the scar I still had over my stomach from the last time I'd seen Duncan.

I followed her into the cold, dark water. My arms floated slightly, buoyant. Hers dropped straight down, and her steps seemed to grow slower and heavier as we got deeper.

"Are you all right?" I asked. "You're not scared?"

She dipped down for a second, head underwater. Stayed down longer than I wanted her to as I scanned my surroundings for someone to ask for help bringing her back up to the surface. But she made it back up on her own. Survived the sinking, the submersion. I realized the spring night of prom—of any big dance—wasn't a climax or an ending.

We shivered at the water's edge and while we made out afterward. Her eyes were bright, soaked stone gleaming in the moonlight.

Clown Faces

I wish I could tell you everything in this world is kittens and laughter. That good intentions always get realized. That people are, in some fundamental way, decent and good. But people aren't anything more than the choices they make.

See Shannon. Wiry little girl with fair skin and short, curly brown hair. The kind of girl who was beautiful if for no other reason than because she had no idea she was even pretty and spent half her time playing with her hair, flopping it over her face to hide from the world. It's always the prettiest girls who mask their skin, who line their arms with tattoos, color their hair with neon streaks, and cover their faces in paint.

I'm getting ahead of myself.

See another girl—I never knew her given name. Tall, with flowing red hair; not the hair people call red that's really orange, but darker, richer, truer. Long, delicate nose; high cheek bones; full lips. The darkest irises you've ever seen and deep circles under her eyes from all the nights she'd gone without sleeping. Worry lines creased her forehead, but her cheeks were uncommonly smooth from rarely smiling.

Shannon loved children. She loved the way they reminded her of simpler times in her own life. She loved that they didn't worry about nuclear proliferation or the debt crisis. That when she babysat, she could slip into the imaginary world of a four-year-old. They were bank robbers. They were police. They were mermaids. Everything changed in seconds and on whims, but she never had to worry about finding her way home. She spent her summers in a lifeguard's chair, watching kids at play, protecting everyone.

The other girl loved magic. She loved to manipulate people into believing what could not be true. She loved misdirection.

She loved to disappear and not resurface because the audience cheered or grew confused, but only when she felt ready.

These two girls had never met, had never heard of one another. But I guess you could say they're destinies were intertwined. Neither would end up the same were it not for the other.

All right, all right, I'm getting ahead of myself again.

Back to the beginning.

The first day at Spiddledy Clown College marked the start of Shannon's new life.

She took a new name. After she was admitted in the spring, she had to submit the new name to the dean's office for approval of its suitable joviality, originality, and pronounceability. In May she received a terse letter confirming she would henceforth be known as Shanaran.

Shanaran rode the train north from Maryland, all the way through Pennsylvania, up to the northernmost reaches of New York State, outside a little place called Shermantown. She missed her train stop because she struggled to wrest the larger of her two suitcases from the overhead storage rack and the train lurched into motion before she could get it down. I giantess helped her with it and Shanaran got off at the next station, twenty miles down the road. Each of the suitcases weighed about as much as Shanaran herself, stuffed as full as a clown car. She dragged them across the platform and followed the signs to the first restroom.

She took a new face. She had to arrive at Spiddledy in paint and after four years, God willing, she would cross the stage at commencement the same way. She had to sleep in paint. After she showered, she would reapply her paint in a bathroom mirror before anyone else could see her naked face.

The fluorescent lights buzzed like bees overhead, casting the restroom in a sickly green hue. She sponged her first coat of paint over her skin, a white base, in the cracked mirror. For a girl who never wore lipstick or eyeliner or rouge, smearing the stuff over her forehead seemed like a revolutionary act. Her skin felt rigid when the paint dried, and she felt sick from the smell. She steadied herself. Excess red paint dripped from her brush. She set to work on her eyes.

A taxi ride, and a haul across campus later, she arrived outside her dorm, a big brick building, the outside covered in patches and crooked lines of moss. It appeared someone had fought the moss for a while, but grown lazy about it and finally given in.

Shanaran met her new roommate—the other girl I told you about—newly named Arabullonia.

Arabullonia was taller and her perfect red hair seemed so much better suited to a clown than Shanaran's boyish curls. Arabullonia's paint was thicker, more even. In the dorm room's funhouse mirror, affixed to one of the neon orange cinder block walls, Shanaran could see on her own cheeks where one stroke of her paint-covered sponge had ended and the next had begun.

Arabullonia gripped Shanaran's shoulders and moved her face close. "I met some boys."

They met up with these boys—Galoofus and Labroni—outside the dorm after dark. The muscular boys wore matching tight black t-shirts. Galoofus was the better looking of the two, with wavy blond hair and wide eyes. Labroni stooped and had his face painted in vertical stripes that made his features look disproportionately long.

The four of them walked off campus together and snuck in the backdoor at a carnie bar called The Three Ring.

We look at people as types. The meek, the strong, the entertainers. Most folks think clowns are here for our amusement, but what of the times when they amuse themselves? They're not so different from the rest of us in their natural environment besides the painted faces, the rubber noses, the occasional toot of a horn. They drink their beers, their wines, and their liquors. They laugh and play games.

Shanaran smelled the peanut shells before she heard the first one crack beneath her foot. The whole place was colored in a soft yellow light, and in the corner, a portly, middle-aged clown played "Thunder and Blazes" on a pan flute. Cigarette smoke filled the empty spaces between mismatched furniture—a plastic patio table with a bite taken out of its side, a long wooden bench that spanned one of the walls, carved with the initials of lovers past and etchings of butterflies.

The Three Ring was packed. Nowhere to sit. They elbowed out enough room to stand together by the bar.

Labroni sipped from a dark porter. The rest drank light beers. "What are you going to specialize in?" he asked the girls.

"I picked comedy," Shanaran said. "It seemed like fun."

Arabullonia plucked Shanaran's beer stein from her hand and took out her black handkerchief, dotted with silver sparkles. She hung a handkerchief over the sides of the glass and waved her fingers one-by-one over the top. She pulled back the handkerchief. No beer in sight. The boys clapped and Shanaran followed their lead. A moment later, Arabullonia dangled the handkerchief in front of the glass again. When she pulled it away, the beer was back, the glass three quarters full precisely as it had been before.

"You're a magician," Galoofus said.

Arabullonia pinched the red circle on his right cheek (a little bigger than the one on his left). "Figured that out all by yourself?"

Never trust a magician. When she gets to be any good, everything she shows you, everything she says is a deception.

Arabullonia clutched Galoofus's bicep every time she wanted his attention; she giggled into his ear every time he told a joke.

Shanaran stared at the reflection of her makeup in her glass, convex, everything coming to a point at her big red nose. She made eye contact with Galoofus "How did you end up at Spiddledy?"

"Funny story. I was studying anthropology at this state school."

"Sounds interesting."

"That's what I thought, too." He puckered his lips when he drank, the same way Shanaran did, probably every bit as afraid of messing up his face's paint as she was. "It turns out it's hard.

And you're not supposed to say something is interesting. You're supposed to explain why it's interesting. And if you give the same reason as some book, then you're either a plagiarist or you're not well read enough for your opinion to matter."

You get these moments when someone lets his guard down and tells you more than he intended to. It usually happens after a couple drinks. When you see someone's truest self, you make the decision to embrace them or to say it was nice knowing you.

Shanaran and Arabullonia each slid closer to Galoofus. Labroni watched a guy across the bar throw darts.

"I'm sorry," Shanaran said.

Galoofus finished his beer. "I flunked out," he said. "Clown College seemed like it might be more my speed."

"I'm eighth generation." Labroni pounded his empty glass against the bar and raised his eyebrows at the bartender. "Every one of us jugglers. And I'll tell you, Spiddledy is no joke."

Pool tables only exist in college towns for two classes of people: boys meaning to lean across a girl's body and girls meaning to let them. By midnight, they'd sipped their third round of drinks and Galoofus had stretched a long arm over Shanaran. He guided the stroke of her cue stick over the purple felt table. She laughed when the white ball grazed the nine, inching it half the distance to its intended pocket. Arabullonia leaned over the opposite side of the pool table. She had loosened an extra button at the top of her blouse. Galoofus didn't seem to notice.

Shanaran stopped after her third drink. Arabullonia had at least three more.

Labroni found a basket of onion rings abandoned at the bar. He bit into the first one and offered them to Arabullonia, who crinkled her nose.

"Let's go over there," Galoofus whispered in Shanaran's ear. The bar crowd was thinning. He laced his fingers between hers and guided her to an empty space on the bench.

No sooner had they sat than Arabullonia bounded after them. She straddled Galoofus in her skinny jeans and her beer splattered over the side of her glass onto his shoulder. "Trying to get away from me?"

Galoofus laughed. "Maybe it's time we all head home."

"But I'm not sleepy."

Galoofus kept the smile waxed on his face even as he planted his hands on Arabullonia's hips to wrestle her off him.

They left. Galoofus and Labroni smoked cigarettes along the walk. Shanaran supported Arabullonia's weight over her shoulders.

At the dorm, Galoofus elbowed Labroni. "It's probably going to take a little muscle to get Arabullonia up the stairs like this. Why don't you give her a hand?"

Labroni seemed all too eager, tossing the butt of his cigarette in the grass and swooping to lift Arabullonia over his shoulder.

"I want to stay," Arabullonia said.

"The party's over," Galoofus said. "I'm gonna finish my cigarette and then I'll go to bed." He put the cigarette in his mouth, the flaming tip pointed at Shanaran. "You want to keep me company?"

Off staggered Labroni, Arabullonia in his arms.

Alone, at last.

"You ever smoke before?" he asked.

Shanaran shook her head. She tried to keep from smiling too widely and wondered if he could even tell beneath the paint, standing in the dark.

"Everybody should try once."

Their hands touched. The first time, when he took her hand at the bar, it happened so suddenly she didn't remember the details -- if his skin was smooth or rough, how far she needed to stretch her fingers to weave them into his bigger hands. The touch was briefer this time, incidental. She noticed he was still warm. The night had cooled off and Shanaran was freezing.

She took the cigarette and inhaled. The smoke felt like sandpaper on her throat. She coughed.

Galoofus took the cigarette. "Not a smoker."

Shanaran coughed more and eyed the row of windows on the third floor of the dorm. She couldn't remember which window was hers, but she had to assume Arabullonia would be in the room by now. In a strange place, drunk and alone; worse yet, drunk with Labroni.

"I should go upstairs."

Galoofus took a long drag and exhaled the smoke through his nose.

She kissed his cheek. "We'll talk soon."

"Good night."

When Shanaran opened the door, Arabullonia was puking her guts out.

Alcohol is a cruel thing.

Shanaran held her hair.

Arabullonia raised her head from the waste basket. "Do you see this?" Her breath stank of vomit. A cluster of red hairs had matted to the corner of her lips. Arabullonia pointed to a corkscrew-shaped scar over her right eyebrow, hardly visible beneath a coat of white paint.

"It was my fault." Arabullonia's shoulders slumped. "I wanted to prove something to my father. I tried a stupid trick with a cloak and a dagger that should've collapsed. But I was nervous—I'm always so nervous in front of him."

Shanaran put a hand on Arabullonia's back. Sweat soaked through her spaghetti strap top.

When Arabullonia at last got up from the wastebasket, she sat at the edge of her bed. "My father didn't want me to come here."

Shanaran retreated to her suitcase and ripped open the packaging to pick out two balloons. She inspected them in the dimly lit room to be sure she had the colors right: one red, one green. From there, she blew three long, steady puffs of air into the green balloon, and four into the red one. In squealing, slippery motions, she tied the red balloon into a four-petaled cross, the green one intertwined at its center.

Arabullonia had toppled onto her side, balled up like an egg, her knees tucked into her chest.

Shanaran crouched at her roommate's side. "My parents divorced when I was six. My dad only had custody on weekends, and it made me miserable." Shanaran put a hand on Arabullonia's arm. "The first time I stayed with him, he took me to a carnival, and I cried and cried."

Shanaran pictured that day, her memory blurry with a child's tears. "My father bought me cotton candy and tried to win a stuffed animal for me with the claw machine, but he couldn't. And then a clown came up to me. He knelt down." She cocked her head to one side and reached out her other hand. The rubber squeaked between her fingers. "He gave me a balloon flower."

Arabullonia opened her mouth as if to laugh, but she didn't make a sound.

"I figured out later that I wanted to be a clown," Shanaran said, "so I could make people happy, too."

Arabullonia took the flower and smelled it. She laughed at herself. "No one likes a clown with baggage."

Shanaran flicked her fingernail against the red balloon, so the opposite end bounced against Arabullonia's nose. Arabullonia laughed louder, sat up, and swung the balloon flower like a club.

Shanaran lay in bed, exhausted. Her head ached with the dull throb of alcohol. The final moments she would remember from the night: Arabullonia standing and leaning over her dresser, pressing the blade of a pocketknife down on something small and white. The tip of the blade caught the moonlight and shone for an instant.

"What are you doing?"

I can tell you, there are seconds in your life that feel like minutes. You ask a question and wish you hadn't because the whole situation feels off and in the passage of time, you realize the person you're talking to either doesn't want to answer or doesn't know how to; she's stalling to find the words or the right lie.

"Sleeping pill," Arabullonia said. "I can't get any rest without it. They're strong, though, so I cut them in half."

Shanaran closed her eyes again, and the last thing she heard was the knife cut through the pill and tap the dresser. She dreamed of boys and balloons and beer and billiards and blades coming down.

#

Their first semester at Spiddledy, they took Carnie Philosophy.

Old Professor Herumpumpum had taught the course for over thirty years. He delivered lectures in the purest sense, uninterested in what his students had said. Uninterested in new ideas. When class let out, no one wanted to talk about content of the lecture; the old professor inspired greater interest in an ongoing debate as to whether the tufts of white on his head were his actual hair or a wig.

One day, he blew his nose into a white handkerchief with red polka dots, a reversal of the color scheme of his sports coat. "One of the central tenets of clown performance," the professor said, "is to wear one's emotions as openly as possible."

Some rules come easier with age. Some cater to youth. You'll see what I mean when you get older.

Shanaran and Galoofus grow closer. They went from furtive smiles and holding hands beneath the lunch table to Galoofus spending the night together. Arabullonia faced the wall and waited each night for the squeak of bedsprings. It never came. The two of them were too chaste. They held each other.

They made Arabullonia sick. If Galoofus was hers she would ride him like she had her father's middle-aged business partner from Bombay. She would let him explore and invade every inch of her the way the way the German diplomat had.

Shanaran and Galoofus crossed ankles with one another beneath the long lecture hall tables in Carnie Philosophy. They wore their love, their joy, their innocence for the world to see.

Arabullonia didn't hide her emotions; just herself.

She disappeared.

There are few sights less comfortable to the lonely than people who are not; particularly people who might've been dear friends or lovers. Shanaran invited Arabullonia to dinner with them, and to the movies. Arabullonia went along sometimes but also gave her roommate privacy. She started taking her pills more sporadically, in favor of long nights in the library reading about sleight of hand and misdirection. She took moonlit walks, circling the big top on the quad or the broken-down carousel outside the president's house. She named each of the chipped-paint horses and pretended they cared. When she was certain Shanaran and Galoofus wouldn't be around, she ate Chinese noodles in the dorm room.

Arabullonia sat one row behind Galoofus and Shanaran in the lecture hall. Shanaran rubbed her calf against Galoofus's skin. Arabullonia alternated between pulling out her hair and kneading her black handkerchief.

Galoofus always took notes. By all indications, he really didn't know a thing about being a clown before he came to Spiddledy. While Carnie Philosophy was mostly rhetoric and review for Arabullonia, it seemed as though every lecture was an epiphany for him.

Herumpumpum sipped from his cup of tea and set it down beside the podium. Every worn wooden table and chair in the room creaked as though it might give beneath the weight of a student, a textbook, a teacup. "Another guiding principle for the successful clown is to always remember it is a clown's job to make others feel joy."

Joy was exactly the small word to embody the small thinking of intro level classes at Spiddledy. Galoofus and Shanaran specialized in comedy, as if pratfalls and dunk tanks required any skill at all.

Case in point: Galoofus's facial expressions. Shanaran described them as the cornerstone of his comedic repertoire. He had tried many and supposedly mastered three: excited, bewildered, and constipated. Arabullonia couldn't tell the difference between the latter two.

"Amidst a clown's myriad concerns, the building block is safety." Herumpumpum blew his nose for thirty seconds straight. Were it any other professor standing at the front of the lecture hall, the class would assume it was a gag. "We look after our own safety so the show might go on. We look out for our audience's safety so they might enjoy the show."

Arabullonia reclined in her chair and tugged at the ends of her hair. He sounded like Shanaran, whose years of work as lifeguard had turned her into a robot. Safety, safety, safety. Safety was all well in good, but no one came to a show to be safe. They came to be engaged; to get so lost in everything they saw and heard that they forgot they were at a show at all. The first rule of entertainment was to take control of the mark's mind.

The time would come. A live performance punctuated each semester at Spiddledy, when the busloads of children arrived and filled the big top's bleachers. The comedy acts would be harmless enough. Fun. Joy. But when it came time to pick the finale of the freshman showcase, surely only the thespians, acrobats and magicians would be taken seriously.

Arabullonia would perform last. She would earn a standing ovation from the faculty, from her peers, and, yes, all of those children, slapping their dirty little palms against each other.

For the time being, she waited. Galoofus, and now Shanaran each took down the lecture verbatim, notes about consistency and care. About sticking to your bit and never letting a child see you with your nose off. Arabullonia sketched pictures of flaming coffins in the margins of the page.

The class packed up. "For the next class, your journal topic will be answering the question, 'Why do you do what you do?'" The usual flurry of hands went up seeking clarification about content and length and format, missing the point that the old professor wanted them to *think*.

For Arabullonia, the answer to the professor's question lay with one of her father's associates. A man from the Midwest who pulled a silver dollar from behind her ear and told her to keep it for good luck. A man who rejected her when she came to his bedroom that night and told her father about her advances in the morning.

Arabullonia hated the man. To see himself as pious, above her wares. Arabullonia's father grounded her, but she snuck out her window and didn't come home for three days. Long enough that she was sure he would worry.

She escaped.

She disappeared.

She was magic.

#

We build up certain moments in our lives. These moments feel like destiny, and yet they also feel completely within our control. We imagine the accolades, the adoring masses. Our lives will never be the same. We think we've earned the transformation.

You never earn a thing in this life that can't be taken from you. Trust me.

The Fall Recital. The students of Spiddledy craved their moment in the spotlight; their opportunity to put their talents on display for an audience of children. For all of the freshmen, it marked the first, truest chance at proving themselves.

Galoofus would pantomime walking an unruly dog through an imaginary park; a dog who chased small children and urinated on a police officer's leg.

Shanaran had borrowed a muumuu from one of the professors, with prosthetic arms on one side, a series of pulleys and levers on the other for her to move the arms to comedic effect.

Arabullonia would lock herself in a coffin and set fire to the lid.

"Absolutely not!" Herumpumpum said. No one had heard him raise his voice before. "Open flames? Around children? And how do you mean to get the lid off yourself without setting the stage on fire? You'll burn down the whole building."

Shanaran had heard the explanations, the answers to all these questions. Arabullonia would line the cover of the coffin with a flame-retardant substance, so once the fire had burned through all of the lighter fluid, it would die down itself. She would spring open the lid as the flames petered out.

Herumpumpum wouldn't listen. "The coffin is bad enough. You do know we're trying to *defeat* the image of the evil clown. And you want to bring death into the equation? I have half a mind not to let you perform at all, you wicked girl."

Shanaran reached for Arabullonia's hand. She would help her come up with a new act. Keep her calm. Reassure her.

Arabullonia stormed off.

Shanaran focused on Galoofus.

"I'm not ready for an audience." He petted an invisible dog, stopping to scratch behind its ears again. One of his professors had advised him to act as though he had the dog with him at all times until it was natural, until every motion on stage became instinct.

"You'll be wonderful." Shanaran hugged him from behind.

"You think?"

"I know."

A group of children from a local school toured the backstage area the morning of the show. The clowns put forth their best faces. Shanaran beamed and waved one of four arms from the cover of her muumuu as the children passed. She was hot in the outfit, and the pressure of smiling and manipulating the arms for ten minutes straight, as every child walked past, wore on her body, her nerves. She collapsed after the last kid was gone, setting her costume on the ground facing the wall, taking her rubber nose off so she could breathe in deeply through her nose.

She set the muumuu on the ground and studied it. Would she be able to hold up the apparatus, let alone perform with it for ten minutes on stage? She had worked out her act with her professor, variations on classic themes. Shanaran wasn't good enough at manipulating the arms to fool an adult into thinking they were real, but her professor said she was good enough that, with more showmanship, she'd have no problem making children believe.

But convincing children her arms were real wasn't what worried her most. She wanted them to like her. And if they didn't? If she was so ill-equipped to engage this audience, did she have any hope of making a life for herself under the paint?

A voice came from behind her. "What's that?"

The voice came from a girl in a bright yellow dress, her hair in pig tails. Shanaran had blown one of the cardinal rules of clowning.

Children may see the puppet dance. They may see the puppet fall, Herumpumpum had said. *But they may never see the strings.*

The girl crouched beside her.

"This is part of my act," Shanaran said.

"What happened to your nose?"

Another blunder. How many times had the professors repeated that a clown's face must remain consistent? That changes had to come between shows, never in the middle when an audience would notice.

Shanaran's foam nose rested on the counter just above the muumuu. Shanaran reached for it, but the girl got it first and studied the thing, almost as big as her palm, a perfect sphere except for a little slit. The slit stretched to fit a small-to-medium-sized nose. The girl dug her thumbs inside.

Shanaran should have reclaimed her nose. Instead, she guided the girl's hands upward and helped her fit the ball on her face. The girl studied her reflection in the body length mirror and laughed.

"A mighty fine clown you make," Shanaran said.

The girl pointed at the muumuu again. "What's that?"

And so, Shanaran showed her how to move the handles laterally inside the costume and how to jerk the one so it would move vertically. "At the end of my act I have a whipped cream pie in that hand, and I throw it into my own face."

"Can I see?"

Shanaran squirted a thick layer of cream over the paper plate and wrestled the muumuu over her shoulders. The pie moved from side to side. Shanaran expected the girl to watch for the levers at waist level. Instead, she followed the whipped cream—the perfect audience—and howled in laughter as the plate flew into the air.

A dab of whipped cream had sprung loose from the plate and arced over, landing beneath the girl's hairline. Shanaran scooped it off and plugged her finger into her mouth. The girl grabbed a handful of cream from Shanaran's hair and shoved it inside her own mouth.

Shanaran put on another nose, took the girl's hand, and walked her to her tour group.

#

I told you about those moments people build up in their minds. The one thing even worse than when the moments come up short, is when they stop feeling like moments at all.

You should be ripe with nervous energy.

You're flat.

To Arabullonia, that old fool Herumpumpum had neutered her act. No fire. No spectacle. No joy.

As a precursor to every recital, the clowns joined the children for a reception. So Arabullonia ate the chocolate cake. The room was bedlam. Children ran from one side to the other. A professor played a ukulele and sang upbeat, off-key songs about otters on teeter totters. Bright balloons and streamers everywhere.

Herumpumpum dressed up like Santa Claus and had children climbing his lap to make wishes.

The whole scene made Arabullonia sick. The hypocrisy of all this brightness and light from a school that censored and criticized and didn't recognize the value of real entertainment. She would get five minutes to perform, relegated to a spot late in the first act, long after the show would have lost the children's attention, and all the little gits would be concerned with was intermission so they could run to the potty.

Backstage, the other first-year clowns wiped frosting and cleared cake crumbs from between their teeth, so concerned with perfecting their appearances before they took the stage. But the children wouldn't notice such things. And the professors? They would give Arabullonia a passing grade because her skill was too great for them not to.

It came time to perform. Arabullonia strode into the theater in the round, lock pick pinned beneath her tongue. She offered her wrists to Shanaran.

Shanaran fastened the handcuffs with care. The girl meant well, but she had no sense of how to sell a dramatic act. Arabullonia wanted the audience to see her as a prisoner. She didn't want the chains wrapped around her arms and torso to embrace her; she wanted them to cut into her skin.

Everything Shanaran did was gentle. She padlocked the chains over Arabullonia's chest. "Is it too tight?"

Herumpumpum cleared his throat over the house mic. "As the audience can see, Arabullonia is chained securely. She will lie in this airtight coffin and, using the sheer force of magic, free herself from all confines."

Arabullonia climbed the steps up to the coffin, on its elevated platform. The coffin was caked in dust when she first saw it. The props manager said he couldn't remember the last time anyone used it. "It might not even be airtight anymore," he had said. People seemed determined to joke around the coffin, as if any joke might change its status as a symbol of death.

"Let's hope it is," Arabullonia had said.

Shanaran climbed up on the platform and held Arabullonia's hands. She'd only picked Shanaran as her assistant for the lack of better options. For lack of other friends.

"As a precaution," Herumpumpum said, "if Arabullonia does not surface after ninety seconds, her assistant will open the coffin to ensure sure the magician's safety."

Ninety seconds. Bullshit. They were supposed to wait three minutes, and Arabullonia had conditioned herself to hold her breath for nearly four. Ninety seconds. If she dropped her lock pick, it could take her half that time to recover it. The bastard wasn't leaving her any room for error.

She sat down in the coffin and surveyed the crowd. All those little faces. While some were distracted -- talking to each other, studying popcorn kernels—more than half paid attention. Enough. The professors watched closely, too. And beside them—

Her father?

Her father sat in the front row, the only one in the theater to wear a business suit. He stared at her, jaw square, legs crossed, hands folded over his knee. He never approved of clown college, and she never expected he would come to the recital?

Her act -- her five minutes in front of an indifferent audience before intermission -- became important.

She lay down. Her breath became short.

Shanaran held the lid, suspended, half-closed. "Are you ready?"

Arabullonia didn't answer. She closed her eyes and tried to forget her father's face. That he was there. That he existed. She tried to release every memory. The ballet recital when she had lost her footing. The speech contests when her index cards had fallen out of order. The time she forgot about the popcorn in the microwave and filled the kitchen with smoke.

But she remembered it all. Memories she hadn't thought of in years. Reborn. Relived in the dark of the coffin.

The chains weighed on her. She couldn't breathe.

How much time had passed? She spat the lock pick out from under her tongue, but it didn't make it to her hands. She didn't hear it hit the bottom of the coffin. God, where did it fall?

She couldn't breathe.

She rolled her shoulders. She knew how to maneuver out of the chains without getting the lock off. A backup plan. A safety measure. She had practiced it a hundred times.

But it was so dark.

She couldn't breathe.

She shimmied one arm free from the chains, but the handcuffs caught and though she was, in theory, closer to freedom, she found it harder to move.

She couldn't breathe.

It was so dark.

Everything went black.

#

No breath. No pulse.

Shanaran tilted Arabullonia's head and pressed her mouth against hers. She breathed in once. Arabullonia's chest rose and fell. Shanaran breathed in again and then set to work on compressions.

I can tell you, there are few feelings worse than the sensation you're moving too slowly but can't possibly speed up. Your rhythm is out of synch with the world.

The big top was silent.

Thirty compressions. Listen. Two rescue breaths. Listen. Thirty compressions.

After her third cycle, Arabullonia coughed. Shanaran's hands shook, one already folded over the other, poised to continue. The EMTs moved in and checked on Arabullonia.

Arabullonia opened her eyes. Teary. Lost. Alive. Some of the paint had peeled from around her mouth, some of it replaced with smears for Shanaran's. Chocolate cake crumbs dotted her teeth.

She was alive.

The crowd erupted.

They fell upon Shanaran. First Herumpumpum. "Marvelous. Simply marvelous. You saved her!"

Then a bearded man in a suit and tie. He shook her hand hard and fast and clapped his other hand hard over her shoulder. "Well done. Thank you."

Arabullonia sat up. The EMTs tried to put her in a neck brace and had a flat board ready on which to load her. She waved them off.

The man in the suit moved to Arabullonia's side. Arabullonia sobbed, open mouthed, the way she had the night Shanaran met her. "I'm sorry."

"You're lucky you had someone to save you." He patted her back and crossed the stage.

Arabullonia fell to her knees.

#

When you leave a place, you always expect it to stay the same. Though time might pass, and ownership may change, you perceive your room, your building, your whole town as your own, and assume you can always come back to it.

Half empty. Shanaran returned to school after winter break to find her side of her dorm room intact, Arabullonia's completely bare, aside from the deflated remains of a balloon flower, tacked to a cinder block wall.

She'd heard winter break freshman year was when Spiddledy had its highest dropout rates. Kids went home, scrubbed their faces, and suddenly liked their skin. They took jobs waiting tables or pumping gas or filed applications to more traditional academic programs at more traditional schools. But Shanaran never imagined Arabullonia would disappear.

Shanaran felt responsible. Arabullonia wouldn't speak to her after her act; wouldn't return her calls over break. Maybe Shanaran hadn't locked the chains around her correctly, or maybe Arabullonia really had a plan, and she hadn't needed CPR and Shanaran had stolen her moment.

"You saved her life," Galoofus said.

Weeks passed. Shanaran and Galoofus talked about Arabullonia less and instead talked of school and childhood and balloons and banana peels and better ways for Galoofus to apply his makeup to accentuate his gifts for facial expression.

In the middle of a study session, lying side by side on Shanaran's bed, Galoofus set down his book. "You're dangerous."

"Why do you say that?"

He touched a hand to her cheek, careful, the same way he had held a goldfinch in their animal training class—too carefully so the bird wound up flying away, flying in circles around the ceiling before the professor could get it down. "Because you're smart. And you're funny. And you're beautiful."

Shanaran touched her opposite cheek. The paint had grown to be so engrained in her life that she didn't notice it when she spoke or when she ate or when she sneezed. But it still felt odd to the touch, brittle and uneven, particularly in those moments when she had forgotten she was wearing any mask at all. "You don't know what I look like."

"Clowns choose their faces." He settled his hand against her face, solid, touching it. His fingers smelled of pickle juice from the spear he at lunch.

"So why am I dangerous?"

"Because I don't know how I'll ever get over you."

Why would he need to get over her? Did Arabullonia leaving make him feel as abandoned as Shanaran had?

Was it a line?

She would never know for sure. Galoofus pressed her, pushing into her hard enough to knock his rubber nose off, then hers. In the overheated, dried out dorm room, he pulled off her hoodie and the tank top underneath, unfastened her bra, and cast them all on the floor. He pinned down her arms as if she fought him.

She hadn't known he had a condom. Hadn't known if he had a plan, but just the same, it seemed inevitable. Where everything was heading. What they both wanted.

He rolled the condom over himself.

They were always covering themselves. Somehow. Someway.

"Go slow, okay?

Galoofus didn't say anything, but steadied himself, working his way up and down rather than bullying his way through. He crept inside as her body welcomed him deeper, as she started to enjoy it.

She didn't realize he had come until after he pulled out. He rolled on his back and lay beside her, barely fitting on the dorm room mattress. He pulled the wrinkled, drooping condom from himself, a half inch of milky white at the bottom, a film of her blood on the outside, and he dropped it on the floor beside their clothes.

"Did it hurt?" he asked.

It had, at first. Then she liked it. Then she felt neither good nor bad, like the sensation of holding anything with any part of her body. It simply was.

She rolled on her side and rested her cheek on his chest, hugging her right arm across him. She pinned her left arm underneath her body. It would lose circulation soon. She'd never be able to stay like that. But for the moment, everything from the smell of his deodorant to the sticky feel of their skin as sweat dried and they cooled off—everything seemed perfect. She let him play with her hair, felt his fingers work their way along the curls from end to root.

"I love you," he said.

"I know."

#

I don't like to tell you about dark places, dark people. I'm not telling you this story to scare you, but because you're old enough to know there are things far darker than the chocolate syrup you pour over a scoop of ice cream. Things more bitter than sweet. Things that really are dangerous.

Arabullonia never went home. She cleared out of the dorm room and ran away with a rogue circus.

She hitchhiked until she found them, north of the Pennsylvania border. They were on their way south for the winter. A Chinese man—the Ringmaster—presided over the operation. He cut his hair close to the scalp, stood half Arabullonia's height, and kept his fingernails twice as long as her own.

The circus toured small towns without permits, never spending more than one night in the same spot. They had a two-headed man; the second head wasn't a prosthetic, nor was it fully functional. The best Arabullonia could tell, the man happened to have the slack vestige of a shriveled second head that protruded from his clavicle. The circus had a bearded woman who appeared to be as much dog as person. The nights of full moons, The Ringmaster recast her as a werewolf, and she howled at the moon. Arabullonia never heard her speak.

A circus such as this would take an unlicensed clown, but no one sought out a carnie who left Spiddledy the way she had -- one placed on such stringent probation, who chose to leave of her own volition. Arabullonia asked The Ringmaster not to check her records. He asked why he shouldn't.

She slept with him the first time that afternoon.

Arabullonia performed magic. She dyed her hair darker and wore gray face paint. She sawed puppies in half. She decapitated herself. She locked herself in a coffin and didn't touch the chains until after she was certain the stagehands had set the lid on fire. No safety precautions. No ninety-second rule.

The Ringmaster let her perform. He let her use props no one else had a use for. He fed her and took her from town to town. They never spoke of money.

When they lay with one another, Arabullonia fingered the scars on his back. Elevated. The size and shape of human tongues.

He was a self-trained lion tamer.

The Ringmaster bartered for Lucille, trading a fire eater and four sacks of potatoes for the creature. The rest of the circus questioned the choice. Why accept a lion without a lion tamer? Why accept a female lion at all?

"Big cat," The Ringmaster said. "All the same."

Every night, children ask their parents the same questions. "Where is the lion's mane?"

Arabullonia wanted to rip their little tongues out and explain how no two creatures were quite the same, and now they had their own scars to prove it.

But she remained still, muted, standing atop the cage until it was time to drag the rope up, hand over fist, to raise the door to Lucille's cage and welcome her into the arena.

Lucille followed The Ringmaster's directions: the crack of his whip, the raise of the hoop, the swing of his arm. Arabullonia admired him at first, a kindred spirit, untrained but no less skilled in his craft. But soon she recognized his lack of artistry; his every movement stilted and rehearsed. Any deviation, any break from the script, and Arabullonia felt certain Lucille would maul him.

After the shows, they set up camp. The Ringmaster, Arabullonia and Lucille shared a private tent. They slept on a blanket over grass or dirt or pavement. Lucille watched them through the bars of the cage. She never slept; they had that much in common.

What did their sex look like to the lion? Did Lucille understand intercourse? Or did it look like Arabullonia were hurting him? If the lion escaped, would she come to his rescue? Or join the attack?

The Ringmaster always took forever to come. His pecker was too small for her feel much of anything. She swiveled her hips, bobbed up and down, then started to pant, to moan, to whimper, to scream. The sound of her fake orgasm was the trigger. He screamed. The lion's roar completed the three-part harmony.

Afterward, he traced her make up with his finger. "Just once, I'd like to see your face without the paint. One day."

"One day," she said. She'd never show him, though. She wouldn't stay with his circus long. She demanded bigger things than to be locked in a cage all her own, left to pace the walls, her only freedom to perform. She had new places to see. Old friends to visit.

After The Ringmaster fell asleep, she locked eyes with Lucille and imagined their conversation.

"I'll let you free when I go."

You trust me?

"You can do what you like."

No whip?

"Go wild."

I'll kill them all.

"Just let me go."

I'll give you a head start.

"I'll disappear, love."

I've found the people who have every reason to be happy never realize it until they lose something. They take everything for granted and then wonder why the world has forsaken them.

People who are profoundly unhappy will do anything to bring the rest of us down to their level. They'll plot and they'll travel, and they'll spring up when you least expect them.

Shanaran had made the dean's list. She had Galoofus. Based on a referral from her advisor, she would spend the summer at an apprenticeship with one of America's foremost balloon zoologists. But in the immediate moment, her every prospect of happiness hinged on the Spring Recital.

The Spring Recital was far bigger than the fall one. It happened outdoors. Children from all along the coast flocked to the show, as did scouts from all the major circuses. Enough cotton candy and fried dough you could smell it across a county in any given direction.

Shanaran and Galoofus planned a joint comedy routine that would combine her skill with his good nature. The afternoon of the performance, she waited on the opposite side of the stage from him. They would each cross the stage and meet in the spotlight.

Arabullonia materialized behind the bright yellow curtain at Shanaran's side. A shock to Shanaran.

Arabullonia's features had grown darker, even her lovely red hair turned black. "You're here!" Shanaran said. A shiver up her spine told her it wasn't right. "We didn't know what to think after you left."

Arabullonia cupped her hand in front of Shanaran, her handkerchief over the top. She removed the cloth with a flourish, to reveal a flower in her hand. "You dropped this."

Shanaran clutched the big white rubber daisy she could have sworn she had attached to her lapel a half hour before.

"You have to be careful with your props." Arabullonia's arms hung limp at her sides. "Remember what we learned in Carnie Philosophy about safety. It's the building block of what we do."

Shanaran re-pinned the flower to her shirt. She shook herself to make sure it wouldn't fall again.

"You leave a prop unattended, and you never know what someone might do." Arabullonia fingered the edges of the flower. "They could empty out your water and pour in hydrochloric acid." She paused. Her eyes locked on the curtain over Shanaran's shoulder. "The littlest bit of acid can hurt someone. And it's not a quick pain. It burns when it first happens. The scar from a chemical burn can last a lifetime. If you sprayed it in someone's face, it could leave him disfigured." Arabullonia pushed one of Shanaran's curls behind her ear. "Good luck."

The preceding performer brushed past them on his way off stage and in that instant, Arabullonia disappeared.

When Shanaran joined Galoofus under the glaring white stage lights, she couldn't see him the way he stood before. She saw him the way he would look, were his face burnt and bent.

Shanaran went through the motions of their performance. Every footstep seemed to pound against the crimson red hardwood floor and echo in the silence of the auditorium. Galoofus stooped toward her flower and sniffed deeply. He leaned away, eyes shut tight, cheeks elevated in his most content smile. He bent to her again, her cue to squeeze the bottom of the bulb and fire the water at him.

Shanaran squeezed his rubber nose instead. The visual was funny enough to draw a sprinkle of laughter from the faculty audience, the ones who laughed at anything to reassure floundering students. The children didn't make a sound.

My God, we've lost them.

They had departed enough from the script to lose Galoofus, too. It took him a full minute of fumbling before Shanaran could cue him for the final motions of their set. She peeked at the crowd. Blank stares. Apathy. Most of the kids didn't watch them at all.

They left the stage to the softest applause of the afternoon. Indifference. Failure. Shanaran cried, and once behind the curtain, threw the flower into the first trash can she passed.

Sometimes we want to know the truth about things. Sometimes we'd just as soon try and forget something as fast as we can.

But you can't forget some things. In the months to follow, when Shanaran closed her eyes to sleep or to make love, she saw the skin beneath Galoofus's eye wrinkled and folded like a Venetian fan. It became his default, his true face in her mind's eye to such an extent that when she opened her eyes to find his white paint smooth, she kissed him harder, held him tighter.

And Arabullonia's face—Shanaran would hardly recall the scar on her forehead or the even white layering she had already mastered when Shanaran was still learning her craft. Shanaran wouldn't remember the way Arabullonia looked when she cried her first night at Spiddledy, or her wide eyes when she held the balloon flower a new friend had crafted especially for her.

Clowns chose their faces. When they stood behind the curtain, Arabullonia's cheeks were colored in silver, her smile as black as charcoal.

Reel-To-Reel

Paranormal Activity *(2007): When a menacing presence haunts them, a young woman's douchebag live-in boyfriend plants cameras around the house to capture supernatural phenomena. The phenomena escalate.*

Ingrid and the rest of the staff all agreed: The Reel-to-Reel video store was haunted. No two ways about it after Big Todd himself, the manager, had seen the toilet flush, the lights flicker, videos fall off the shelves—all without anyone close by enough to hold responsible.

When Big Todd was convinced, he took measures to track what was going on. Cameras in every corner; it was the latest technology, motion-activated. Ingrid only recognized then, when looking up at the lens of the camera by the Horror section, that it matched the little convex, black glass circle—like the pupil of an enormous eye—at the front counter. She'd never realized Big Todd monitored the cash register and the person working it at all times.

"Of course it's monitored," Gabby said through smacks of her bubble gum. "Big Todd doesn't trust anyone."

Ingrid didn't know that side of Big Todd but had intuited bits of it based on the regular coupons he awarded her for *perfect drawers*—the exact change she was supposed to have at the end of a shift at the register. The free rental wasn't much reward when employees got free rentals anyway. She passed them on to her parents, who never rented movies, until they overflowed the kitchen junk drawer. But then, Ingrid didn't think of a perfect drawer as a big deal, besides suggesting others were miscounting or stealing.

Gabby was capable of unethical behavior. On the premise of a smoke break, she disappeared outside a few times per shift, and during night shifts when Big Todd wasn't around, she'd disappear for full hours. Ingrid felt certain Gabby'd ridden off with her boyfriend those times, only to be dropped back off in time to close. One time, she came back with a cherry slushie, not trying to hide that her disappearance had lasted longer than a cigarette. Another time, she brought a slushie for Ingrid, too, green apple. Slushies were too sweet for Ingrid, but it was a nice gesture, so she decided she liked Gabby, even if she didn't much like her boyfriend who only came in the store when Big Todd wasn't around, and who was cavalier about pulling free rental coupons from a whole pad of them Ingrid could only assume Gabby had stolen for him.

Big Todd didn't like Gabby. He put up the cameras on the premise of catching a ghost or demon, but Gabby said in no uncertain terms that all he meant to do was watch them all.

For all the mutual disdain between them, Ingrid struggled to place why Big Todd didn't fire Gabby, or why Gabby didn't quit. Mostly, Ingrid tried to stay out of it. She tried to see the best in Gabby and Big Todd alike.

Ingrid applied a similar logic to the ghost, too. It might not be a malevolent force so much as an old friend or relative to someone who worked at the store, or a lonely specter of a cinephile who waited until movies she wanted to see got rented out so she could go home with the renter and watch them.

Still, late at night, alone in the store, hours after Big Todd had gone home and the staff was down to Ingrid and Gabby, and Gabby, in defiance of the cameras, stayed out on her smoke break as long as usual, it was harder to lend the benefit of the doubt to shadows moving in the stillness, the creak of the floor without any customer to set foot on it.

Maybe everything was in Ingrid's imagination, but these bits of haunting kept her at the front of the store where the lights were brightest and where she'd experienced minimal paranormal activity.

Ingrid waited until she couldn't wait any longer for her fears to subside or for Gabby to get back. She had to pee.

She moved down the aisles at a half-run, as fast as she could without looking like a child or a lunatic if Gabby did come back, or Big Todd stopped in, or if they actually had a customer at that late hour on a school night.

No tapes flew off the shelves at her. No disembodied voice whispered her name. She made it to the bathroom OK, and she peed and peed and peed while she caught her breath.

Seated there, she noticed the black, glassy pupil, half hidden by the paper towel dispenser.

Big Todd was watching. Footage at his disposal for as long as he meant to keep it.

#

Weekend at Bernie's (1989): Hapless men do their best to convince everyone a dead body is still alive via assorted shenanigans and contrivances. It mostly works.

Big Todd found Ingrid's body in the wide space between the aisles of Comedy and Horror films at the Reel-to-Reel video store. Watching along, as a specter, Ingrid felt some relief at having been discovered. As miserable as it might be to see Big Todd react to finding her dead, and as devastating as it would be for Ingrid's mother and father to hear the news, things were at least in motion.

Only they weren't.

Big Todd checked her pulse.

Big Todd rested a hand on her chest.

Would he try CPR?

Would he call the police?

He looked both ways and lifted her body. He tried to cradle her, one arm behind her back, the other beneath her legs, but stumbled and dropped her, knocking her skull against one of the steel shelves. He tried again. A modified fireman's carry over his shoulders but stooped low so no one could see he had her.

Why didn't he want anyone to see?

Shouldn't he have wanted help?

Big Todd brought Ingrid's body to the front of the store and seated her on the tall, swivel chair where employees sorted returns. A customer made his way to the counter with three DVD cases and a box of Milk Duds. Big Todd got behind the chair and crouched.

"How are you today?" Big Todd asked, a high pitch to his voice that sounded nothing like Ingrid's. Of course, this customer wouldn't know Ingrid's voice.

This customer didn't show any signs anything was amiss. Making the small talk. Mostly concentrated on wrangling his fat wallet out of his too-small pocket and extracting the laminated Reel-to-Reel membership card, too wide for the slot in the wallet he'd wedged it into.

They completed the transaction, Big Todd going so far as to lift Ingrid's arm and position her thumb and forefinger to pinch the card and hold it, to swipe it on the register.

Maybe the effort of moving her body was too burdensome, or the game of it had worn thin after the first customer. After the customer left, Big Todd set Ingrid's body to rest, arms folded over the front counter, head rested on them, so her face was covered. He cracked jokes to the customers to follow about how she must have had a hard night, or how ordinarily he didn't let employees sleep on the job, but clearly she needed a nap. They laughed politely in response, no one looking closely enough to notice Ingrid's body wasn't breathing, no one questioning what Big Todd had told them.

When Ingrid's shift was over, Big Todd took her body home.

Rather, he took Ingrid's body past home, lingering outside her house long enough to catch her mom as she came home from the grocery store. Big Todd lifted Ingrid's arm and waved. Mom waved back, distracted, and headed inside.

Ingrid's mom would have noticed when Ingrid didn't come home. Assuaged, Mom wouldn't notice Ingrid was gone now until the next day. Maybe two days?

Big Todd took Ingrid's body to his place.

He put her body on the couch and popped in *Ghost*. He sat next to her, his arm touching her arm as he ate off of leftover pepperoni and green olive pizza. The pepperoni like sores. The olives like pussing blisters.

And as he rested his head in her lap, dinner done, in the late stages of the movie—as Patrick Swayze got behind Demi Moore to mold the clay on the spinner one more time—it occurred to Ingrid how easily Big Todd had taken all of this. Yes, it was strange he'd spend this day with her body, but even more so that it all seemed so rote. Almost as though he'd known what to expect. Almost as though he'd planned it.

He dozed off, as drool bubbled from between his lips to leak on her body's jeans. Ingrid screamed at herself to wake up.

Please, wake up.

#

Paranormal Activity 2 *(2010): The plot is more or less the same as* Paranormal Activity, *except this one's set as a prequel with more exposition, so it all makes more sense.*

The key to a good haunting is to start subtly. Go for the big scare too soon and everybody runs away. Focus too hard on one person and you'll drive him crazy, which isn't *beside* the point, but isn't the appropriate place to start either.

Ingrid haunted the Reel-to-Reel video store. She mostly meant to haunt Big Todd.

The trouble was Big Todd was surprisingly unflappable when it came to the supernatural. He brushed it off when people complained the DVD player at the front of the store played spontaneously, no matter how gruesome the gore-fest Ingrid carefully arranged to broadcast. He wasn't troubled when the microwave in the break room started up unattended or when the ceiling fan gently blew over the store without anyone turning it on.

Whether it was the sheer volume of complaints from the staff—not least of all living-Ingrid—or the time Ingrid flickered the lights just right after Big Todd had turned them off, such that it visibly gave him pause—he finally responded to the haunting.

He put up cameras.

The cameras felt as though they were courting a scare. Daring Ingrid to confirm her presence.

It made Ingrid angry.

It made her angrier when she followed Big Todd home. He reviewed the tapes, no clear indication if he were even looking for anything paranormal, so much as he fixated on living-Ingrid, Gabby, and the other women who worked at the store, going so far as to freeze the frame and peel back the elastic waist band of his tighty-whities with his thumb and smile.

Then he put a camera in the bathroom.

It made Ingrid angry.

Living-Ingrid discovered the bathroom camera for the first time. The moment of paralysis when she meant to cover up, futile because the camera had already captured her there, and whether it caught her for a second or an hour, Big Todd would nonetheless own that image of her.

Living-Ingrid didn't say anything about the camera. She almost talked to Big Todd about it but stopped short for fear of confrontation. She came closer to telling Gabby, but faltered because Gabby would tell Big Todd living-Ingrid had told her, or else quit before she said anything at all. Living-Ingrid liked Gabby and didn't want to risk her leaving.

It made Ingrid angry.

Big Todd watched the bathroom tapes and smiled.

It made Ingrid angry.

It made Ingrid angry.

It made Ingrid angry.

She threw a shelf of new releases at him when he walked in the store. Steel crashed against the linoleum floor. DVD cases everywhere. A cobweb of broken glass where a corner of the shelf caught the front window.

She'd missed Big Todd. Maybe because she couldn't bear to actually kill him.

It made Ingrid angry.

But she was tired.

And though the big shelf and its big fall gave Big Todd pause, it wasn't a big pause. And he didn't go back to watch the tapes of how it had happened.

Truth be told, in the immediate aftermath of the shelf flying at him, as the cacophony settled from metal and plastic and glass crashing in their turns, Ingrid could have sworn he smiled.

#

The Ring (2002): A girl bound to a video tape calls viewers and kills them seven days after they watch her.

All Ingrid wanted was to get at Big Todd.

The trouble was getting the video in his hands.

She thought it'd be easy. He kept a tub of VHS tapes and DVDs behind the counter—films on the verge of being retired from the Reel-to-Reel video store—took them home when the tub was full, and ritually watched each one to determine if it were worthy of returning to the shelf, better added to his personal collection, or trashed.

Ingrid didn't care if he liked her movie, only that he watched.

She suspected after the requisite seven days had passed and she mauled him, she'd be free. That's why she remained on earth, wasn't it? Confined to a video tape in a video store? Big Todd was the work left to be done.

But it took time.

Ingrid stared back at a string of renters through the screen, who seemed puzzled, maybe a bit disconcerted by what they'd seen—more so by the follow-up phone call. And yet they dutifully rewound the tape, put it back in its case and returned it to Reel-to-Reel.

Ingrid felt poorly for a woman—probably as young as Ingrid when Ingrid had died. The woman dropped her glass of Chardonnay when Ingrid blinked on her screen. The woman cried when she got the call. She clutched the tape afterward in shaking hands, and Ingrid worried she'd unspool it, try to break the thing. The woman put it back in its case and backed away, though, leaving it atop her TV. Ingrid waited days there, while the woman started to accrue late-return fees, while it became possible the video would never find its way back to Reel-to-Reel before the woman was dead, and there Ingrid would remain trapped, her best chance resting on someone returning her to the store after they cleaned out the apartment.

But the woman collected herself enough to bring the tape back.

After seven days, Ingrid made short work of her. Cutting to the quick. As few scares as possible. Static, out of the TV, blunt force, and back in.

Finally, an opportunity arose.

Ingrid had lost track of the months, maybe years gone by. But an office worker in his twenties brought her home and popped her in the VCR while he loosened his collar, watched while he ate the leftover half of a meatball sub, cold from the fridge.

If the man were frightened by the movie or the call, he betrayed no sign of it. But the next morning, he brought Ingrid back to Reel-to-Reel before work and handed her straight to Big Todd at the front counter, telling him the movie was mislabeled. "That's not *Top Gun*"—finally, someone had noticed!—"It looks like some kind of art film."

Big Todd apologized and gave him a voucher for a free rental of any non-new release. After the man left and after Big Todd had studied the unlabeled tape for a moment, he did the most remarkable things of all. He set her down in the tub of movies to take home.

It's not only that Ingrid went in the tub, but the tub was already full, so she perched on top of the tape of a George Carlin stand-up routine and *Beaches*. Not only was she leaving the store with Big Todd, but the tub was full enough that she'd leave soon and for her position on top, he might watch her first.

He took her home that night.

Ingrid could smell Big Todd's car then in a way she couldn't the last time she'd been in it. Pickles and tuna, maybe a dash of horse radish. Cool Ranch Doritos, all decaying by degrees.

He carried the tub from his car through his front door.

And he tripped.

The rug was uneven, and a cat scurried when he caught himself, slamming his foot down hard on the ground. Tapes spilled from the tub.

He muttered that the cat was a bastard as Ingrid slid under his couch. Judging by the dusty cheese puffs and cobwebs, the feathered cat toy, she was out of sight, or at least out of reach for Big Todd and the cats.

It was dark there.

Maybe Big Todd would find her. His curiosity sparked by the suggestion she was an art film, he'd search for the tape. What art film would Reel-to-Reel carry in the first place?

He watched George Carlin.

The next night, he watched *Beaches*. Ingrid could've sworn she heard his breath falter when Bette Midler sang "The Wind Beneath My Wings."

He moved on to the next tape. The next DVD.

And the next.

And the next.

It was dark. Cold. Cat hair drifted in now and then. Ingrid could smell Big Todd's farts.

All Ingrid wanted was to get at Big Todd.

Her muse for murder.

Her only hope.

She waited.

She wasn't going anywhere.

It's a Wonderful Life *(1946): After a long, miserable life, a man encounters an angel who shows him what the world would look like without him.*

"You've been given a great gift," the angel said. "A chance to see what the world would be like without you."

The angel said this as if the world were so different. But at the Reel-to-Reel video store, it all looked the same. The same center display of Holiday Favorites with *Die Hard* moved over from Action; The *Muppets' Christmas Carol* from Family; *The Family Stone* from Drama; *Home Alone* and *Scrooged* displaced from the Comedy section.

Gabby still wore the elf ears and red and green striped hat Big Todd the manager didn't like. Little Todd, high as a kite, languidly vacuumed the same patch of carpet over and over.

"You've been given a great gift."

A girl materialized. Her name tag read *Cecelia*.

Big Todd stood near, leaning over her when he could justify it, to point at where he envisioned the New Year's display with sparkling cider and *When Harry Met Sally* and *200 Cigarettes* would go up for the week after Christmas, when folks were sick of Christmas movies and Christmas decorations and Christmas songs.

Big Todd smelled Cecelia's hair. When no one else was in the back of the store, he took her sunflower butter and blackberry jam sandwich from its Tupperware, peeled back the top piece of bread, and put his tongue there. Later, he watched her eat her lunch in the break room.

"You've been given a great gift."

Big Todd took a break shortly after Cecelia's shift ended. She hummed along to "Jingle Bell Rock," windshield barely defrosted enough to see through. The car smelled sweet like cinnamon.

Somehow, Ingrid was in Big Todd's car, too. He blasted his defroster hot in his eyes and kept his headlights off despite the fading daylight as he followed Cecelia home.

"Is it a gift?" Ingrid asked the angel. "To know the world would be the same, only another girl in my place."

"You've been given a great gift," he repeated. He was broken, maybe by this circumstance an angel wasn't equipped to process. Maybe an old model, expiring in front of her.

Cecelia didn't return to her parents' house like Ingrid would have. She drove to a dodgier part of town where she shared a studio apartment furnished with a futon and a card table, lit yellow by a desk lamp, where her live-in boyfriend had made scrambled eggs and white bread toast to dine on. He was taller than her, skinnier than her, with a tattoo that read *you're breaking my heart* down his forearm.

Big Todd watched them, car expertly parked behind a tree that kept him out of sight, a set of old school, almost comically oversized binoculars trained on their window. He'd watch for a long time, Ingrid intuited.

The angel started to tell her she'd been given a great gift, but she cut him off, understanding it was time for her to tell him she wanted to live again and to run down the street in corporeal form celebrating a return to the world she knew, incontrovertibly influenced for her presence in it. That's how the story goes, even if her desire to live again was limited to keeping someone else from having to suffer the same consequences of a close working relationship with Big Todd.

But the angel was still stuck on telling her she'd been given a great gift.

She saw through Big Todd's binoculars. Cecelia kissed her boyfriend and fetched fast food ketchup packets for the eggs.

It felt warm in the car.

Ingrid couldn't get out of the car.

The angel was gone. She was stuck with Big Todd as he fetched a bag of Cool Ranch Doritos from his glove compartment and ate what was left and tilted the bag to pour the crumbs down his gullet when he was done. Ingrid could taste the salty ranch flavor and the speckles of it tickled Ingrid's throat as they did his, so they coughed in unison until wads of Dorito dust phlegm made it out of their mouths and splattered the steering wheel, where they shimmered in streetlight refracted by the frost on his windshield.

Big Todd started the car. He had, apparently, seen enough. Ingrid stole one more look at Cecelia, oblivious, touching her finger to a silver bell in her foot-tall fiber optic tree by the window.

Ingrid was stuck to Big Todd. The roads were slick, and he slid a few inches past the line at a red light and turned on the radio while he waited for it to turn. He sang along to an old-timey version of "I'll Be Home for Christmas."

The light flashed from red to green, Christmas colors, faster than it seemed like it should have, a bit of holiday magic. Big Todd drove back to the store. Reel-to-Reel stayed open until deep, deep into the night.

Bet Your Life!

The mechanics of *Bet Your Life!* were simple enough. It looked like a slot machine. It played like a slot machine. The only variation was that rather than feeding quarters through the slot— there was no slot at all—you bet an arbitrary percentage of the life you had left to win. You win some, you lose some. Unless you bet big. You win big enough, you might live to a hundred and fifty—at least that's what I figure. You lose big enough, you'd better have your affairs in order.

I never asked for *Bet Your Life!* and I probably should have turned it away when it showed up at my door. My father'd taught me life was all about calculated gambles. Before I was born, he bought out a failing newsstand and repurposed it as a snack bar. When business was thriving and Mom was pregnant, he closed up shop to renovate and expand, doubling up the size of the joint to put in seating. Called it Saul & Son's, after him and me. He made a calculated gamble. To sacrifice some immediate business in favor of the long-term, and to count on invoking a child to compensate for business he might have lost for changing the name of his enterprise.

I'd gambled bigger when I installed slot machines as soon as the state legalized them. After Dad's stroke, after I'd inherited the business, the demand for a local snack bar dipped, and I needed an edge. The slots worked, too. Kept me afloat.

But *Bet Your Life!*—it's not something I planned for or needed. It seemed like a low-stakes gamble.

The machine had its name splayed across the front of it in bubbly yellow letters. I told the delivery man he must be mistaken—it had to be intended for a slots parlor in another town or the casino an hour west. Not my snack bar where, day by day, even having slot machines in the business my father opened up to sell ice cream and hotdogs to neighborhood families turned my stomach, and one by one I kept considering pulling all the plugs and making it a family place again, rather than a home for the local degenerate gamblers to while away their afternoons.

The delivery guy didn't seem interested. Clad in a brown collared shirt somewhere between business attire and work clothes, and a pair of matching brown shorts. He had calves as thick as my neck. "This is the address." He pointed the stylus to the address on his tablet. "You can refuse delivery, and it will go back to the vendor."

"Who's the vendor?"

He sighed, scrolled on his tablet, and showed me that, too. *Games, Inc.* Not my usual company. About as non-descript as it gets. *Address withheld* printed beneath in brackets.

I kept the machine. I probably shouldn't have, but what the hell? A new game, free of charge to pique the interest of the regulars, maybe get them to drop some extra change, and if they liked it maybe they'd spread the word.

Shelly studied the game with me after I'd plugged it in. Slots are supposed be simple, nothing more than receptacles for money. You feed in cash. Pull a lever. Every few spins you get a couple bucks back. Or you don't. Repeat, repeat, repeat until you're bled dry.

But I couldn't figure out this damn machine. No spot for loose change, or even a voucher like a lot of the newer machines called for (a trend I had resisted because I figured it would confuse people, not least of all me).

Shelly smelled like lavender. I liked her and liked any excuse to interact with her. She wasn't like the degenerates, though she was the daughter of one. She came in after work to look after her father, Old Man Withers. He had wandered in from their house across the street after he moved in with her. The first day, she came in after him, panicked, and I thought she might be one of those hysterical people who yelled at me for letting him gamble, then hauled him off never to be seen again. But she seemed to like that he'd found something to entertain himself, and I could only assume she was the one leaving quarters for him to play. So, I saw them both about every day. I poured her Diet Cokes gratis, and I listened to her bitch and moan about how backwards her office was, stuck in the 1950s where men still asked her to get up from her reception desk to make copies so they could stare at her rear end. We agreed she should search for a new job, though as far as I knew, she never got around to it.

Together, we crouched at the base of the new machine and leaned around its side. No directions or payouts anywhere. She suggested maybe it could be a prototype for a game on the way, or a novelty machine kids could fiddle with while their parents gambled for real.

I'd never heard of anything like that, and people who made these machines were into the business of penny counting and number crunching enough that I had a hard time believing they'd make something to give away for free.

"Why don't you try playing?" Shelly asked. "See what happens?"

"How?" I smacked the side of the machine, hard enough my fingers smarted afterward.

Shelly was gentler. She reached past my stomach and pressed the white *BET ONE CREDIT* button, then *SPIN*. All the slots were built to look like you could play them without paying any money. One of the tricks to lure folks in. They see how fun it looks, but they can't play. The machines don't give you free plays—even with nothing at stake—because the manufacturers recognize even that might be thrill enough to satiate the gambler's need, betting on air. I knew it wouldn't do anything when Shelly hit the spin button.

But it did.

The five reels whirred to life. All the images were generic castoffs from rejected game concepts. A river. Rocks. A desert. A goblet.

Shelly got three straight rocks. A digital display beneath *LINE PAYS* flashed and produced the number *3* in red.

She spun again. Lost all three credits she'd earned and the phantom one she had started with. Then spun again. The thing kept going. Maybe the company had pre-installed some free-play or, unlikely as it seemed, the machine had come to us pre-owned, and someone hadn't played out every quarter they put in. But then, there was no indication of how many credits she had anyhow.

She positioned her fingers over the button that read *BET MAX CREDITS*.

"You sure you want to do that?" I asked.

She hit it.

Five reels. The first four showed rivers.

PAY ONE HUNDRED CREDITS.

She lifted her hands over her head and screamed as though she actually had won something.

"Too bad you can't cash out," I said.

Shelly flashed me a grin. "You get what you pay for." She stood close to me for a second. I'd have to get a stool for *Bet Your Life!* if people were going to play it, but maybe it was better not to invite anyone to linger too long on a machine I wouldn't make any money off. Heck, if people played it enough, I might start losing money in electricity. Shelly stood close and I could see the shape of a wavy black line, rising above her collar, up toward the back of her neck, the top of a tattoo. I'd never pegged her for the tattoo sort, and it felt like something special for me to be aware, a secret she was letting me in on.

Old Man Withers elbowed past me to edge in on the machine. I stepped aside, right into Shelly as it turned out.

"Eager, are we, Mr. Withers?" I started in.

Shelly pressed her palm to my chest. It's funny how once you touch them it seems altogether more reasonable to touch them again, especially when you're still standing right there. I studied her fingernails, uneven from biting. She spoke softly. "Leave him be."

My hand found its way to her hip, her face mere inches from mine. Withers bet the max credits and won—three wings in a row, forty-five credits. He played again and lost. Then again, another loss. Tried to play max credits a third time but the machine didn't budge. He tried again and again. Nothing.

Withers jabbed his finger against the button a couple times more than the one credit button, hard enough I worried he might break the machine or hurt himself.

So, I intervened. "It's a new machine, Mr. Withers. We've still got to work out some kinks. Why don't you go play something else while I give it look."

He squinted, forehead wrinkled like he got lost in thought or suspected a machine owed him a jackpot it hadn't paid, but he wandered off.

I studied *Bet Your Life!* and for the hell of it, pressed my finger to *BET ONE CREDIT*. The reels spun for me.

I lost.

#

I didn't want to admit the rules of the game. That a man might really bet away his life on something as silly as a slot machine.

But in a small town, any death at all is cause for news, and as I scrolled through the morning headlines, I read about the passing of Terrence Withers. I got hit with that compulsory sense of one's own mortality, a deep-seeded twinge folks feel past a certain age, whenever they hear about anyone else dying. The sensation was followed by a bit of wistfulness about not seeing the old gambler around my place anymore, and, worst of all, a pang I might not see Shelly at the snack bar again either.

That day, my only customer was The Kid—a regular whose name I'd known and forgotten, but it didn't seem to matter much. He was there three or four days a week but never hit the snack bar itself, never offered more than a nod of salutation my way, just moved from machine to machine, most days working his way through a whole roll of quarters.

After all those emotions settled themselves, I got to thinking about the slot machine and how it wouldn't work for Old Man Withers after he lost it all, but it would still work for me. I thought I was crazy—who wouldn't? I probably still would have if it weren't for Shelly coming back and speculating along the same lines, only surer of herself.

Shelly scanned the place at mid-afternoon, earlier than she usually came around, because of course she was off for bereavement. The Kid was feeding the last of his roll of quarters into the *Double Diamonds* machine. Besides him, these two old birds who stopped in every now again.

"It's the fucking machine," Shelly said. "Dad was old, but he wasn't sick. I made sure he took his meds. He bet the max and now he's gone."

I might have dismissed it as the bargaining step in the grieving process, but what she was saying added up. I could feel my adrenaline pumping—that sensation of working with a mystery on someone. Better yet, working with Shelly, when she didn't have any make-up on, when she wore a sweatshirt and smelled like sleep and tears, like she hadn't showered or brushed her teeth, and she was letting me in on something almost criminally intimate. Because she'd come to me. Because, in her hour of need, we were together.

We started speculating what the maximum bet meant if you were, in fact, betting your life. The minimum bet? Were we talking years? Months? Percentage of time remaining?

I got called away from our conversation because the biddies wanted refreshments. I'd constructed the story in my head that they switched off from their regular bingo game every few weeks to play something riskier, but they never showed much interest in talking with me, so I never confirmed it. I had to get one of them her popcorn with extra butter—her order every time, and I had to quietly follow her around wiping down the machines she played because she smeared butter on the buttons. She spent more time picking out of her teeth with her fingernails than she did on the slots. The other was focused, though. Changed ten dollars when she came in and never left before she'd spent it all. She bought a king-sized root beer and a carton of peanut M&Ms.

I thought Shelly'd either be halfway through her next theory or she'd be gone by the time I was done with the old-timers. I couldn't expect her to stick around on a day like that, but I understood it when she changed a five-dollar bill in the machine and sat down at *Pot O' Gold.* I remembered when my father died. I went to be with my mother but after a few hugs, tears shed, and reminiscences, we were on the brass tacks of when the funeral would happen, where we would have the reception, and making burial arrangements. From there, we got to the small talk two people have after they haven't seen each other in a while. *I like that color on you.* and *Is that a new rice cooker?* and *Have you seen the commercials for the new show with the people who get trained to chop the heads off snakes?* I'd puttered around the house a couple hours before I excused myself and wound up at a bar—not even one I had any sentimental connection to; some place new I hadn't remembered seeing before. I ordered a double and picked at my cuticles. Someone dies and you figure the whole world is going to stop, but it doesn't, so you keep passing the time, figuring you ought to have something better to do, the mundane infringing on your innate sense everything ought to be different.

I had a hard time figuring if Shelly wanted me with her—if she were waiting on me, even—or if, under the circumstances, she wanted to be left alone, so I gave her time, restocking soda cups and lids and getting a rag ready for old popcorn hands.

I didn't notice it when The Kid found his way to *Bet Your Life!* It probably would've taken me longer if I hadn't checked on Shelly and caught her watching him.

I got as close as I could without crowding him, to see what would happen. He won and lost and won and lost and started betting the max credits. If you're not gambling for anything anyway, why wouldn't you? He lost, lost, lost, lost, lost. The machine froze up on him the way it had on Old Man Withers. Shelly dug her nails into the vinyl on the back of her seat. The both of us were frozen in that space of knowing we ought to say something, and knowing we'd sound like crazy people.

The Kid tried to bet one credit, but that button quit on him, too. He shook his head, got up and walked straight out the door.

Shelly rushed to the machine pressed *BET ONE CREDIT* and sure enough, the reels spun for her.

She looked at me like she was going to say something about how this machine was the devil, and we ought to throw it from a bridge. Or about how we ought to chase after The Kid and warn him to look out because his number might be up.

I'll never know what she was going to say, because the both of us turned around to look out the glass storefront at the sound of screeching brakes, just in time to catch public bus C1 slam into The Kid's body and send him sprawling five feet straight back, the front of him crushed on impact.

#

Shermantown, New York is known for snow. The winters here are long and cold. It's not atypical to get a hundred inches of snow in a season.

The Kid got hit by the bus in autumn. We would rarely see snow much before Halloween and still had weeks to go. For whatever combination of reasons, the way people filled up the street reminded me of the way snow would block roadways, all but paralyze the town before the municipal plow came through.

It started with a flurry. People running from storefronts. More people than I ever imagined patronized the businesses of Main Street on a weekday afternoon. People saying somebody had to call an ambulance and everybody assuming someone else had until it became clear minutes had passed, and no one called for help. The bus driver, an older man stuttered about how The Kid stepped in the road, in front of the bus. "Maybe he wanted to kill himself."

People filed off the bus. Some took pictures. Of the body. The bus. The driver. The surrounding businesses. They followed the path The Kid must have walked from the sidewalk. Right from the doors of Saul and Son's.

The bus driver got on the bus, and for a second I thought he meant to drive away—a catastrophically stupid attempt at a hit and run. One of the passengers must have thought the same. A wiry woman with an ill-fitting mess of a curly black wig who hollered for him to wait.

It turned out he wasn't going anywhere, just getting on his radio to call for help.

The media got there ahead of the police or the ambulances. They were looking for eyewitness accounts. This one with a steno pad. That one talking into a microphone, a cameraman with a bulky, outdated camcorder stacked on his shoulder.

Did anyone know The Kid's name?

Was it really an accident? The bus driver got indignant, pointing at the transit crest embroidered over his heart and talked about twenty years of safe driving until the reporter clarified that she meant to ask if it was a suicide.

Where was the kid coming from?

That's when folks started asking me questions. Was The Kid playing slots? Did he lose? I saw the writing on the wall. A problem gambler and the proprietor of the slot parlor hadn't had the decency to ask if he was OK. This was the flipside of running slots in a town without any competition. I had the only place for gamblers to go, but a host of righteous bible thumpers had stopped patronizing my business when I installed my first machine. A little ammunition and they'd run me out of business.

I mumbled something about how The Kid came in sometimes, and I noticed he seemed distracted. He'd even bumped into Shelly and hadn't seemed to notice. She squinted at me like she was trying to figure out what I was up to but nodded along slowly.

I was worried they'd storm my business. Team up to haul slot machines down to the floor and kick them until they were beyond repair. Maybe one of those machines would land on somebody's foot and they'd try to sue me. But while there were those people who glared at me and a reporter who lingered for a few more cursory questions about The Kid, things diffused. A woman was talking about calling out to The Kid when he stepped into the street. A man complained about spilling coffee on himself when the driver slammed on the brakes.

I suppose that's what happens when there's a tragedy. A kid gets hit with a bus and you'd expect it to bring everyone together, but before long it's all about each of their individual experiences of the event, like the way people want to tell you where they were when they heard about JFK or 9/11.

So, I slipped off, back into Saul and Son's. Shelly came back, too, shell shocked. She sat in the same seat where the old birds had abandoned their soda and popcorn to be a part of the scene outside.

Then I saw her. Blond girl with letters spelling Littlewood Community College spread out across her neon pink sweatshirt. Real pretty. The kind of girl I'd have had a crush on back in school, or who'd make me linger while I was channel surfing late at night, long enough to hear her voice, to get a sense of her story. She wandered past Shelly, and via whatever magnetic pull the game had, found herself in front of *Bet Your Life!* After a second of study, maybe looking for the coin slot, looking for rules—a second when I know I probably should have said something— she pressed the button to *BET MAX CREDITS.*

Shelly held her breath.

Blondie won. Of course she did.

Ordinarily, if someone wins on her first pull, you can be sure she'll pull again. Some folks know to quit while they're still ahead, but you'd be surprised how many folks keep going. Because if they win once they'll win again. Because they imagine they can win back everything they've ever lost in their lives with a little luck, as long as they don't give up.

This girl was smarter. She walked away from the machine, out of the snack bar, out of my life.

I pulled the plug.

I broke one of the cardinal rules of the slots game. You *never* pull the plug. Someone's on a hot streak? You let her ride it out and lose back her winnings. Someone's losing more than he should? He's an adult, making his own choices. You must look out for your profits. Every quarter is part of the lifeblood of your business.

But everything about this game was different.

The police arrived outside. More than enough to close off the street and tend to the body outside. A place like Shermantown, there's not much for officers to do so they turn up en masse if there's an incident, grateful to have a mob to tend to. Afterward, a positively pubescent kid whose thin, scraggly facial hair—a goatee in progress—wandered in and asked me what I knew about The Kid. I said the same half-truths and lies from outside, which he wrote down dutifully in his little notebook.

Shelly got up and left.

The officer glanced at *Bet Your Life!* conspicuous for being the only machine turned off, and I worried he might ask me something about it, because it seemed so obvious to me the machine should be the subject of interrogation. But the moment passed. He shook his head and told me to have a good day.

#

I closed up shop for a few days, but still came to work to stare at the machine.

In the end, I hid it. I couldn't bring myself to throw away *Bet Your Life!*—nor could I leave it out there for anyone to play. So, I wedged my own dolly underneath it and carted it behind the counter and past the crates of popcorn kernels and soda syrup, back by the freezers where only I would ever see it and where, upon testing, I positioned it just close enough to reach an outlet.

I'm not sure how, but word got around about *Bet Your Life!* People didn't show up in droves or anything, but now and again I'd get inquiries from people who'd heard I had a special machine. Usually, I acted like I didn't know what they were talking about. One cited The Kid. That time, I admitted I'd had it but told them I'd sold it off to someone who made me a good offer, someone who paid me well enough not to disclose where he'd taken it.

One time, I was really tempted to let someone in back. A guy with a black toupee, no eyebrows, real skinny and frail, dressed in a blazer. Who knows how he heard about the machine, but he told me he had traveled a long way to see me. "I need to play," he said. "Money's no object."

Who was I not to let him spin the reels a few times, or if money really was no object, who was I not to really sell him the damn thing?

But then, who was I to let him have it? Giving someone a chance at life or death felt too much like God. I'm just a guy whose dad ran a snack bar. A guy who brought in slots to make an extra chunk of change.

I told the man he was out of luck.

Shelly came by again. I poured her a Diet Coke.

"I thought the sodas would only keep coming as long as Dad was losing money," she said.

"One last one." I winked at her. "For old time's sake."

She didn't wink back.

She didn't say goodbye either, but between how little she did say and how long she took to drink her soda, I could guess she wasn't going to come back unless I gave her a reason to. Unless I said something.

But I evaluated my prospects and the odds. The joy of striking up a conversation that might lead to one dinner which led to a whole lot of dinners to follow. Maybe we'd get back to exploring *Bet Your Life!* like a couple of kid detectives.

I thought about losing. What did I expect when our only connection was death? Ten-to-one, things wouldn't turn out well.

Someone looking from the outside in might speculate eventually I'd make a move. Given enough time living in the same small town, one day I'd knock on the doors of all the houses nearby until I found her, or out of sheer happenstance I'd run into her, feel the weight of never taking my chance before and finally say *something*. But that's why romantics make poor gamblers. They're the kind of people who don't realize diligence never pays at slots. If a man insists on playing at all, the best bet is to make only one spin. Every spin after that, the lopsided odds compound on each other. In the long run gamblers always lose.

Slots are a sucker's bet.

Every now and again, after I close and finish wiping down the machines and the counter, after I take the trash out back, I plug in *Bet Your Life!* I never bet the max. I take it slow. I never bet more than I can afford to lose.

Take Me Home

For years and years and years I lived at home. I took care of Mother after Father's accident, and it's only ten months now since she died on my twenty-ninth birthday, almost peacefully, aside from the bit when she writhed and could barely be held in place at the end. Cody told me that's normal.

Cody helped me sell the house—after we removed the wadded-up cash Mother had hidden in the walls, of course—and now Cody and I live in his apartment. He calls me tangerine and banjo, anything with an *anj* sound, and I giggle. I like it because my name is Angie and he makes me feel like I own these words, and I've hardly owned anything in my life. That's changing, of course. We own a big television now, and I own new dresses, and we have money enough to go on adventures. I'm not supposed to talk about the money, though.

For a while, I was worried all adventures would ever mean were trips to the old glove factory. I do love that place, for the smell of old leather and all the boarded-up windows, but I've visited two dozen times and know the scares better than the guides now. I caught one who misnamed the man who hanged himself after he was laid off for being a drunkard. *Carl Strowman,* I said, *not Bowman.* The tour guide—who I recognized immediately as Bob Cratchet from the Shermantown Community Theater production of *A Christmas Carol*—glared at me and I was frightened. I wanted Cody to stand up for me, but he stepped around so I couldn't hide behind him anymore and put an arm over my shoulders. He said, *Angie knows her history* and everyone laughed. People aren't supposed to laugh on ghost tours. And then everyone knew my name, including the ghosts, and they whispered *Angie, Angie, come to us, Angie* for every room we walked through, and I didn't like it at all. I haven't gone back to the glove factory since.

But here we are now, on one of our adventures. We're driving east and, my goodness, across state lines. We passed into New Hampshire. "I've never been this far," I say.

"Really?"

I giggle. He knows I rarely lie and he's teasing me. I like it far better when he teases me than when the ghosts do, or when the girls at school did. At first, I thought Cody was mean like them, but Mother told me boys act mean when they like you, and it turned out she was right, and when I told him he was a cretin he laughed and rubbed my arm until the goosebumps went away.

The sign says *Welcome to Purville*, and signs rarely lie, so I take it to be true this is the name of the town we are visiting. We drive for thirteen minutes before we pull into a motel, and we could afford to stay in a nicer place, but Cody always says that's how the wealthy lose their money—through frivolous spending—and we can have our fun, but we also ought to conserve.

The walls of the room taste like cigarette smoke, even right beside the gold placard that says *Thank you for not smoking*. I tell the sign, "You're welcome," but someone must have broken the rule sometime and now they've gone and spoiled it for the rest of us, because I don't much like the smell, much less the taste.

Cody tells me to leave the walls alone. "Bundle up," he tells me next. He has put on his new wool coat and wrapped his neck with the gray scarf I knitted for him last Christmas that I'm also so pleased to see him make use of. "We'll be outside for a while, my little tangent."

This adventure doesn't take us to the glove factory, but it does still involve ghosts. He we're bound for a haunted pub crawl, where we'll go from place to place and have drinks and hear ghost stories and it sounds wonderful.

I wear Father's old winter coat that reaches my ankles and swallows up my arms in the long, baggy sleeves. Mother always said I should have it taken in if I were to insist on wearing it, but I didn't want to change a thing about it and cursed at her when she washed Father's smell from it, but fortunately it came back after a few days. Now it smells like him and me and it's about my favorite thing in the world.

We walk to the meeting spot, outside a red brick building with perfect rows of glass windows inside, some lit, some dark, like the way a scab takes shape in blotches and with rough edges, no pattern to it at all unless you cut yourself very, very particularly.

We wait. The first ten minutes are fine, but then I started to wish I'd known before we left Shermantown that we would be outside for so long. I would have brought my earmuffs to wear under my wool hat. It must be negative twenty out here. We're only fifteen miles from the Atlantic, Cody said when we pulled in, and I can feel the ocean, with all its freezing death encroaching on me. I wonder if there are ocean waves this time of year or if they've frozen into sheets of ice.

For a while, it's only us. We might have gone to the wrong meet-up location if Cody misread the instructions like he does sometimes, though he always insists he's right. But then more people arrive. An ancient couple with yellow wax in their ears. A bald, fat man with a big camera strapped over his neck. Two pretty, blond girls in purple sweatshirts with Greek letters over them. They smell like lavender and they're the only ones Cody says hello to. I give him a look.

He says, "Relax, my vegetable mél*ange*."

I giggle.

A man arrives next. His hair gelled into place, neatly parted down the side, and he looks like someone from another century. He's deathly pale and wears a pea coat over a button up shirt. I suspect straight away that he is a ghost, but then maybe he's our tour guide, and this is a trick. He doesn't announce himself, but maybe he's like one of those mean tour guides from the glove factory who mill around and rile us up about our guide being late only to reveal himself, and everyone laughs except for me, because I recognize he's wasted our time.

As I'm about to tell Cody about the man and what he's up to, another man arrives, who's shorter and has the big feet and disposition of a circus clown. He leans in close to me and inspects me with a monocle. He has a corncob pipe gritted between his yellow teeth and smells of tobacco and alcohol. His clothing is much like the ghost man, only more wrinkly, as though he slept in it. I don't like him.

He leans away from me and bellows, "Welcome to the Purville Haunted Pub Crawl! My name is Samuel Jenkins the Third, but you may all call me Sam." He withdraws a roll of red tickets from his coat with the flourish of a magician, but none of the grace. He's not good at his job. "As advertised, your tour comes with one free drink ticket per person. But, particularly on a blustery autumn night such as this, I find the tour is more enjoyable when we are all good and sloshed." He winks conspiratorially toward the old man who doesn't seem to understand he's being acknowledged. Perhaps the whole of New Hampshire is dimwitted. "So, I'm going to hand around a few extra tickets, and I won't tell anyone about it if you don't." He rips off tickets, three, four, five at a bunch and pass them out among us. I hope he'll give me four at least, though six would make me the best. He gives me three. I might kick him in the shin if he slights me again.

He not only gives the girls in purple five tickets each but rips off a couple extra tickets for one of them, and says conspiratorially, "Enjoy yourselves, ladies."

The ghost man stands apart from the rest of us and waves off Sam when he tries to give him tickets. I like this apparition.

Sam spins on his heel, and he looks much grimmer than before. "I suppose you did your research and have a sense of where you're standing now."

I try to catch Cody's eye. He's not good about following directions and I wonder if we were meant to do research before we came, and now everyone thinks we're classic fools. He's studying the Greek letters emblazoned over the purple girls' chests.

Sam lays a hand flat against the red brick. "This apartment building used to house all of the workers from a fish processing

92

plant—the men who cleaned, chopped, portioned, and canned everything shipped out of Purville. The men and their families."

There must be dozens of ghosts inside. Maybe hundreds. I'm so excited and I hug Cody's upper arm as he stifles a yawn.

"There was a man who moved up from Florida when fisherman work dried up, too many people casting lines up and down the coast," Sam says. "He got a job at the plant. Dragged his young wife with him north. She was pregnant by the time they reached Purville, and it seemed like as good of a place as any to raise a family."

The old couple leans in close. The man is having trouble hearing and I want to tell him, *clean out your ears, you old dolt!* But Mother taught me not to say such things, only think them. So, I think it very hard.

"They didn't count on the cold winters. His wife wanted to go home, but they didn't have the money, plus the man knew this job could provide for them in perpetuity. So, they stayed on, and the wife stopped going outside at all." Sam shakes his head. "The baby was stillborn."

Maybe this isn't a ghost story at all. Just a sad one. I can feel my throat stick like it's coated in caramel. My eyes fill.

"What happened to the couple?" the old woman asks. She must be a plant.

Sam sighs. "The woman dove from their window." He points upward but it seems he can't bear to look. From where I'm standing, his finger is pointing between two windows on the fifth floor. I want to ask him which one, or if a third window were hidden in brick—a whole apartment bricked up to bury dreadful memories. "She landed headfirst in this exact spot."

"And the man?" the old woman whispers.

"He took himself to be cursed," Sam says. "Maybe he was right. The next time he found work fishing, his ship was lost at sea. None of the men were ever found."

A breeze blows in, hard enough Sam has to catch his top hat from falling off of his head. I shiver at the breeze and nestle into Cody. I think it's Cody, at least, but his chest and body are stiffer than I expected and when I turn around, I discover it's the ghost man who turned away drink tickets. I tell him I'm sorry, but he doesn't seem to mind.

Sam dashes ahead and leads us around the corner of the building before he grandly steps on some sort of pedal. Fog bubbles from two jets I hadn't noticed at the base of the apartment building. Knee high, thick enough so I can't see my feet. It's a neat trick.

"Let the tour begin!"

Cody claps his hands. "Bet your bottom dollar, this is going to be a great tour."

I put a finger to his mouth. We aren't supposed to talk about money.

The walk to the first pub is miserable—cold, uphill, and Cody walks ahead with Sam, and I can't hear anything they're saying.

We come to O'Toole's. It's small and dimly lit. The front window rattles with the wind and I worry it might give way and stab us all with shards of broken glass. The bartender wears a puffy, pastel blue winter coat that looks like you ought to be able to tear pieces of cotton candy from it. She has the skinniest neck I've ever seen, dirty blond hair tied back in a ponytail—the kind Mother would call sloppy and make me fix before I went outside.

Sam orders a double shot of whiskey, but the bartender tells him the drink tickets are only good for wine and beer. They squabble before Cody inserts himself.

"Let's make that two double shots of your cheapest." He brandishes a twenty-dollar bill. Brandishing money doesn't seem so different from talking about it, worse even, but I know Cody won't like me correcting him in front of his new friend.

Sam and Cody are friends now. They drink their whiskey quickly—before the poor bartender has finished pouring for the rest of us, and Cody demands two more. I puzzle over a drink menu and tell her to go ahead and help them. I always have the hardest time deciding. I don't much like beer, but maybe I must try more of it, like how I didn't like popcorn, but then Father bought kettle corn at the fair one evening and it was glorious, and I've eaten it every chance I get ever since.

The purple girls guzzle their wine and are done before I've ordered. Now I'm falling behind. They order different wines this time. How do they make up their minds so quickly? Cody waves them over and splits his tickets between them. He says he won't be needing them tonight.

The old man and the old woman sip off the same beer. The man with the camera takes pictures of something on the wall. Perhaps he sees some spirit drawn to camera lens. I wish Sam would get on with his stories so I could know for sure.

The ghost man stands beside me. He's more handsome with some light on him, his jaw strong, the stubble on his cheeks and chin dotting him attractively. If I were a fairy, I might spend a full day hopping from nub of hair to nub of hair.

I lean against the bar and slip into him. He's not like those ethereal ghosts in Shermantown; he's made of man more than mist. Solid as the bar itself.

"I'm Charles." He reaches out a hand to me. I don't like touching people skin-to-skin much at all besides Cody, but Mother said it's rude to recoil when someone else tries to shake your hand or when someone you know tries to give you a kiss on the cheek and we mustn't mustn't mustn't be rude.

I shake his hand.

"What's your name?

I might tell him *any* name—Jennifer, or Alexandra, or even *Francine*, but my own name tumbles loose, "Angie," and now he and all the ghosts of New England must know who I am and that gives me a chill.

"You aren't going to drink?" he asks.

"I haven't made up my mind yet." My fingers fidget. I hate it. Mother used to take pictures of me fidgeting and she asked me if I thought it looked becoming, and no I did not, so I've tried to stop, but it's so difficult. I fold my arms tight across my chest and bury my hands and remember a good trick my father used to use at restaurants when he didn't know what to order and he'd lean over to the next table and ask what they were having and if they liked it very much. The ghost man—Charles—isn't drinking anything so I'll have to improvise. "Do you have any recommendations?" Perfect, perfect! Well done, Angie!

"I only drink scotch." Charles eyes the meager collection of bottles behind the bars. Not nearly as many bottles as Unlucky Ned's, the bar where Cody has taken me back home. This place isn't nearly as good. "I don't suppose you like Scotch?"

"I do." I've never had Scotch, but I won't admit to anything I haven't done. I don't have to. I see Cody avoid such truths all the time, when he nods along to friends talking about changing the oil themselves on their cars, though I know Cody brings his to the mechanic, or when he deflects questions about the fortune we must have made from Mother's house—questions from friends and my cousin and the mean man in a suit and tie who showed us a badge and said he was from the police. Cody's very good about not talking about money and I'm trying to learn from him.

But scotch, yes, I will be a scotch lover.

Before Charles can go on, Sam starts up. He's standing on one of the bar stools now. The bartender motions that he really ought to come down, but he pays her no mind. "O'Toole's is no stranger to spirits," he says. "Indeed, spirits have come to visit on the regular."

It's a pun. He's raising a glass of whiskey, a spirit itself. He and Cody and I are the only ones in the bar to understand the joke. Only Sam and Cody laugh.

Sam finishes his drink and lets the glass drop to the bar quite carelessly. "One night, a ghost walked into this bar." I think he's telling us a story and I listen closely. But as ghost after ghost in this story get beers and don't pay for them, I can tell—before he even gets to the punchline—it's a joke.

Cody laughs loudly enough at the end of it that it hurts my ears. He's turned pink in the face. I don't like him when he turns pink. The man with the camera laughs, too. The old woman laughs, and then the old man either comprehends the joke late or doesn't want to be left out so he starts to laugh, too. The purple girls appear confused.

I don't laugh. Charles doesn't, either, though I'm quite sure he gets it because he doesn't seem dimwitted. He and I came for a ghost tour, not for jokes. We want to hear stories, and this disrespect is only going to make the ghosts angry and that's when they become dangerous.

Cody takes a step toward me but not to me. Closer to where I stand but his destination is the purple girls, and he explains the joke to them. I position myself so he can't help but see me with my arms folded tight. Mother told me I look cross when I stand like that, and that is exactly what I wish to communicate to him in this moment.

Cody switches from the purple girls to me. "Just a minute, my little evangelist."

I don't giggle.

I order a glass of Chardonnay and give the woman my ticket and tip her with a twenty-dollar bill for putting up with Sam's tomfoolery and because now I don't much care about what Cody would tell me I shouldn't do.

The wine is bad. I drink it fast.

Charles tells me he has a collection of scotch at home. Cody has his back to me. One of the purple girls laughs at last, her hand on his upper arm.

Charles tells me his apartment is only a couple blocks away.

#

Charles lives in an attic above an old woman's house—a proper space for ghosts, though there aren't chains for rattling or white sheets to hide beneath.

The attic reeks of kitty litter, a pastoral, earthy, animal smell I've loathed since I tasted a bit at Auntie's house and Mother told me I was a wicked fool and I spent the rest of the afternoon crying in a corner while the mean tabby licked himself and stared me down in mocking victory, for no one called *him* wicked or a fool.

Sure enough, Charles has a cat, too. He scoops her up and tells me her name is Aglet after her favorite food, and I don't know what an aglet is, but I'm too afraid to ask because Aglet is already eyeing me suspiciously from a perch on Charles's shoulder. She flexes her claws in my direction. A warning.

Charles sets down Aglet, and Aglet rolls over to expose her belly as if she expects a rub, but he ignores her. "Where did you come here from?"

From the pub, of course. But no, he means before. Before the hotel even. "From New York."

He half-grunts, half-laughs, and perhaps he's pleased I've answered his question correctly, though how would he know? No, he misunderstands me. "What is it about city people wanting to get away to our quaint parts of the country?"

He assumes I'm from New York City. Father used to say people thought everyone from New York was from the City, and of course he's right. I decide not to correct Charles—that not only do I live seven hours north of New York City, but I've never been there. "I do love Coney Island." It's a very good response. He'll never know.

He leads me to a shelf with a dozen glass bottles. Labels that say Springbank, Highland Park, and Macallan. He picks up a pair of glass tumblers from behind them all, clutching each in one hand. His hands are enormous. And powerful. And all these bottles and glasses must be out of Aglet's reach on the shelf, or I can only imagine the beast knocking them over, making a mess shining sharp shards. "See anything you like?" he asks.

"I'll try the Glenmorangie." I read the name from the label. A poor selection. I might have gotten the pronunciation all wrong, and he'll call me an idiot.

"Excellent choice." He pours a glass for each of us, only a third full. Stingy, but I remind myself we only met this evening, and these are nice things, and he doesn't have to share at all.

We clink glasses and I giggle, because it seems so formal, and
Cody and I never do such things. I drink too much at once and
it burns terribly, but I'm a good girl and I purse my lips and don't
cough once.

"I'm taking over as tour guide," Charles says. "In case you
were wondering about my clothes." He waves his hand down his
torso. "In case you couldn't tell, Sam is pretty checked out from
the job."

I breathe through my nostrils. The burning is starting to
lessen. I'm beating it.

Charles finishes his Scotch and pours himself another. He
takes a sip from it and then walks behind me. He's got a record
player there. He drops the needle just so and it plays a song that
sounds old, with violin strings and man with a beautiful voice
singing over them. *Crooning,* Mother would call it.

And Charles is kissing me. He kisses my forehead softly.
Then my cheek. Then my lips. Then my neck. Then he pushed
Father's coat to the side so the sleeve hangs to floor and he's
pulling my shirt to the side and he's kissing the base of my neck.
Then my collar bone. He's edging toward my shoulder.
Stretching the neck of the shirt. And he's holding me close to
him. He's so strong. But his kisses are so soft. Soft and warm, no
ghost after all.

But he doesn't smell like Cody. He smells like kitty litter.
And my shirt's beginning to tear, and he doesn't notice. And
Father's coat is on the floor now and it's getting dirty with dust
and cat fur and whatever other filth this man has cultivated, and
his stubble is too rough on my skin, and

NO, NO, STOP, STOP! I HATE THIS AND I HATE
YOU I HATE YOU!

He stops.

I drop my glass on the floor where it shatters.

"I hope you got your money's worth." Charles's voice is low
and mean now. "Damn tourists."

I'm not supposed to talk about money.

I wind up alone on the street. Orphaned. I remember we walked up hill to get from the bar to his apartment, so I walk down hill and before I know it I'm back on the main drag with all of its businesses. I applaud myself. Clever girl, figuring your way back. There's a candy store with marshmallow rabbits in its window and I want one, but the lights are off which means the store is closed. The nasty rabbits taunt me from inside and I warn them that their window wouldn't be the first glass I broke tonight, and they ought not dare me.

It's cold. I'm tired. I walk until I'm close to O'Toole's and before I can decide if I want to go back inside, the band of tourists—the photographer, the old couple, the purple girls, and last of all Sam and Cody—are filing out to the sidewalk. Cody misses the half-step outside the door and stumbles. I worry he's broken himself, and wouldn't that be a fine topper to this exhausting night? But no, he rights himself and laughs.

I go to him. Hug him tightly, because I'm sorry I was gone for so long. Surely, he worried after me in this strange town full of strange people and places—full of strange ghosts, too, I'm sure, though they haven't yet shown themselves. I hope he isn't cross with me for leaving.

Cody wraps an arm around my shoulders. He's tall and this feels good. Like I'm sheltered from all of New Hampshire's evils. "Did you enjoy your drink?"

I think he means the scotch, but how could he know?

He's not asking about the scotch, not asking about the apartment. He never noticed I was gone.

"Take me home, please." I nestle my nose into his chest. He smells like Cody and that's good. When he doesn't respond right away, I repeat the "Please."

He sighs but says all right. When I'm truly not feeling well, sick or sad, he takes care of things. I admire that about him and it's one of the reasons I trusted him from the start.

I want him to take me all the way back to Shermantown. Back to Mother's house. Even though it isn't Mother's house anymore, I'm sure those walls would still remember me and still soften at my touch, still taste of sweetness. And my bedroom would shift and bend and rearrange. It would become mine again. All of these things I'd lost might come back.

Cody staggers. He's too drunk to drive, and I'm not allowed, so we'll only go so far as the hotel tonight. I suppose that will do.

He calls back to his new friend Sam, and I think he might want to meet him tomorrow before we leave New Hampshire. I couldn't bear to spend another minute with this man, but maybe it won't seem so impossible after a good night's rest. Mother always said a good night's rest solves most things. Mother was rarely wrong.

Answer Woman

There were benefits to knowing the answer to every question. For example, when Answer Woman's brother said, "You know you can trust me, right?"

She knew the answer was No.

Edgar ran a hand through his greasy, gray-flecked hair and tried again. "Will you regret spending time with me?"

"No."

The answers surprised her at times, but she had learned to trust unpredictability.

She had not anticipated either of her brothers would find her that spring morning--she didn't know she had siblings then. She had emerged from her fusty, linoleum-covered apartment at dawn to take the number 5 Train to the Metropolitan Museum of Art. But they found her somehow, sitting cross-legged on the museum's marble steps holding a two-foot scrap of cardboard that read:

ANSWER WOMAN $13

She sold her ability to answer any question and to convey it precisely. The ability dawned on her at the age of twelve, when her adoptive mother had asked her if she knew what adopted meant. Without thinking, Answer Woman had said, "It means you smothered your first baby girl with a pillow, and five years later you couldn't have another," and got smacked across the cheek with a spatula still sizzling from the hoecake her mother was frying, banished her from the house.

On the sidewalk outside the museum, break dancers twisted and posed. A magician pulled a mourning dove from his sleeve. Their cries for customers clashed, adding to the clamor of honking horns and random shouting. Answer Woman subsisted as a part of this community of street performers and apart from them.

A man with wire-hanger shoulders approached. Lanky, and with cheekbones as sharp as an arrowhead, he stood so he shaded her from the sun. "Are you the Answer Woman?"

She lifted her head to face him and nodded.

A brown weed stem bobbed between his yellowing teeth. He looked like an extra from an old Western. Answer Woman hadn't noticed it at first, but another man, both shorter and scrawnier, stood behind him. The smaller man was hunched over, his elbows dug into his gut. He smiled like he was caught in a daydream and hummed to himself.

The thin man smelled of whiskey. He wore a wrinkled, off-white banded collar shirt. "She's prettier than I expected." Dirt caked his ridged fingernails. He plucked the weed stem from his mouth and extended his hand to shake Answer Woman's, wincing for a second, clutching at his ribs. "If you're the Answer Woman, that would make us the Answer Men."

He said his name was Edgar and called his smaller, older brother Butch. "We're searching for a missing clue that could help us understand something larger."

Butch rocked and carried on with his melody, the buzzing from his lips growing louder. Answer Woman asked about his humming.

"I've asked him about that myself," Edgar said.

"What did he say?"

"That they are answers to questions people haven't asked."

Butch smiled. He stopped humming for a few seconds.

"Have you ever asked yourself where your power came from?" Edgar asked.

"I don't ask myself questions," Answer Woman said. "I never know the answers."

Edgar snapped his fingers. "Me too. And believe it or not, it's better that way. That's how Butchie got into trouble. He practiced until he could answer his own questions. Once you go down that road, it's like standing at the edge of a cliff. Lean too far and there's nothing to keep you from falling, and no way of climbing back up." He swung his hand through the air, the motion of a judo chop. "You and me, we only go as far as somebody else asks us. But I can see you're skeptical. You want proof I'm for real. So go on, ask me questions. Unload on me."

Answer Woman was more accustomed to the flip side of this proposition. As a matter of policy, she'd answer, free of charge, one question of little consequence in order to authenticate her ability. In the past two days, she'd told a visitor the name of his aunt (Carmen), a firefighter his buddies' codeword for an apartment grease fire that killed more than a dozen people (a skillet of fried chicken), a librarian the seventy-sixth word of *Lord of the Flies* (broken). When a customer agreed to the fee, Answer Woman would then answer the money question.

Now she focused on a man peddling knock-off Vera Bradley purses on the sidewalk, who had fashioned a pothole in the street nearest him into a sub-shelf for clutches. He wore an oxford shirt with a paisley tie. A red cloth hung from his back pocket. "There's a man behind you selling bags. What color is his handkerchief?"

Without looking, Edgar said, "Red."

"What color is his necktie?"

"Paisley. These are easy."

"How many interlocking designs are on his tie?"

"One-hundred-thirty-seven." Butch provided the last answer. He gnawed a strand of calloused skin from his chapped lips.

Edgar smiled. "How many designs, total, does he have on his tie?"

"One-hundred-thirty-seven," Answer Woman said.

"You're as sharp as Butchie," Edgar said. "I can see colors; I can see words. But you ask me for a number—I see all the designs, but I need to count them."

Their abilities proven; Edgar went on to explain that the three of them were blood siblings. "Butch always said we had a baby sister. I was too young to remember someone was missing. Our parents had to give us up for adoption–"

"Stop."

Edgar rubbed his jaw. "You don't want to know where you came from?"

Answer Woman had wanted to know for a long time. She once took a lover from the same town where she had spent her early childhood—Shermantown, New York. She asked him about the place as though she'd never heard of it before and listened to the rhythm of his speech and the way he applied short vowel sounds regardless of the vocabulary at hand: *I lauv Shermantown, and I'd raz a family there. But for Chrisssack I'm twenty-five, I ned a nit liff.* Her lover told her about the way his neighborhood, Miller's Plain, had transformed after the glove factory closed when he was in junior high. It used to be a place where neighbors chatted while mowing their lawns or shoveling snow from their driveways in the evening after work. Things changed when people skipped town, when they had to commute to assembly line jobs thirty or forty miles away, or when they worked swing shifts, mopping department store floors and restrooms, and didn't arrive home until daybreak. *Tack about a city that never sleps.* Answer Woman knew from the start this man wasn't a good match for her, but they drank Malbec, and she bade him to ask her questions about her own experiences in Shermantown. Her eyes throbbed with every answer. She saw the glitter of broken glass and felt jagged edges at her fingertips and at her throat. She thought for sure she'd bleed to death when her lover stopped asking her questions, when he showed her she wasn't bleeding at all. They never spoke again.

The extent of what she knew for sure about her past was trapped inside the glass dome of a snow globe, the weight at the bottom of her rucksack for every move she had made. A town captured in miniature–with winding streets and open pastures beyond a glove factory, a tavern called Unlucky Ned's, a redbrick elementary school, a Greyhound bus station at the edge of the town limits–pressed against the thick glass. A banner stretched

106

across the bottom, identified the place as Shermantown, New York. Underneath, in pink cursive, read, Rose Cakes, Inc. When she was younger, she imagined people wandering the halls of those buildings, and she wondered what Rose Cakes might be.

A few weeks earlier, after a particularly busy day on the museum steps, she'd bought herself a long-stemmed rose and a marble cake from the bakery across Fifth. When she got home, she crushed the bulb in her hands and pushed the remains into the cake. She scooped the pieces in her fingers and devoured the delicate petals, the swirly crumbs—a rose cake all her own.

"Some questions are better left unanswered," Answer Woman said.

"So don't ask them," Edgar said. "Ask only those you need answers to."

Asking Edgar about her past seemed safer when she didn't have to depend on the answer alone, but on a person's memory. "Why did our parents give us up?"

"Our father was a first-class scumbag." Edgar pressed the weed stem with his fingertips, as if he were working out the notes on a flute. "That's what comes to mind, not the answer I mean to tell you. From what I can gather, Mom and Pop thought Butch was a child prodigy. He knew the answers to every question he got asked at school, equations only a budding Einstein would've known. I'm talking calculus here. Big vocab words he couldn't have learned. But Pop catches on Butch isn't really smart, but that for some reason he knows things he has no business knowing. So, the old man brings him to bingo at the Methodist church and asks him which card they ought to play. Lo and behold, they win the biggest pot of the night. He takes Butch to the trotters and asks him which nag he should bet on. Wins that, too. Then he takes him to the gas station to buy a lottery ticket."

"He was exploiting him," Answer Woman said.

"The prick claimed he was looking out for the family," Edgar said. "Mom was seeing an expensive shrink and taking Pop to the cleaners with the bills. But she said no child of hers would be used like that. Then he started testing me and Ma smashed a window–”

“That’s enough.”

Edgar nodded. “I get it. Baby steps. That’s good. We can come back to it later.”

“How did you find me?” Answer Woman asked.

“The truth is, we weren’t exactly searching—at least I wasn’t. I never believed we had a sister. Then we’re standing outside the museum and my stomach’s grumbling. I’d spent my last dollar buying a stem from this crazy fucker in a cowboy hat. I see a guy playing three-card monte on a TV tray on the corner. So, I ask Butchie boy, what’s the easiest game we can run to make ten, twenty bucks here on the street?” Edgar tapped Butch’s wrist. “He says we should do what our sister is doing at the foot of the stairs.”

The men left her alone. Answer Woman hadn’t expected they would, certain they were looking for money or a place to stay, their claim of brotherhood was a scam, or Edgar meant to sleep with her. But after another half hour of talk, Edgar asked Butch if they should continue. Butch said no. Edgar said she should take time to digest what they told her, and he’d see her tomorrow.

Answer Woman went about her business. Five more paying customers had required her services by nightfall. After the last one, she made her way home.

Two years earlier, the city had put bright orange traffic cones at either end of her street and then stripped the asphalt roadway to deep grooves for the purpose of repaving. They took the cones but never came back to resurface the street, leaving it full of uneven chasms.

Answer Woman stopped at the hotdog cart on the corner, where a skinny Jamaican in dread locks stood each day, compulsively clad in brown corduroy pants. She made her typical order. One plain hotdog. One with a dab of relish and a mess of hot sauerkraut.

108

When she first moved in, Answer Woman thought she would make friends with Miss Gwendolyn, the elderly woman next door, but her neighbor never returned her hellos, and the most she would say was for Answer Woman to mind her own damn business when she tried to hold the door for her so she could maneuver her walker into her apartment while she carried a bag of groceries. Miss Gwendolyn made her way inside, slammed the door, and turned a series of seven locks behind her. More often than not, they crossed paths when Answer Woman came home from her day's work and Miss Gwendolyn made her daily pilgrimage to the hotdog cart.

When the City stripped the road, Miss Gwendolyn didn't see it coming. Indeed, it became clear her eyesight was shot, and she promptly fell in the street. Answer Woman helped her up. Miss Gwendolyn didn't thank her, but neither did she take a swing or curse her out. She even let Answer Woman escort her to the hot dog cart and back up to her apartment.

Answer Woman started coming home earlier. Early enough to buy a hotdog for the old woman, repeating the order verbatim about "a dab of relish," "a mess of hot sauerkraut." She knocked on Miss Gwendolyn's door and heard the old woman shuffle to the peephole, then ask her what she wanted. Ultimately, the old woman unfastened all the locks, leaving only the chain in place, so Answer Woman could hand the steaming frank to her. After the third daily iteration, Miss Gwendolyn said she didn't want her stopping off at the cart just on her behalf, so Answer Woman started tucking her cardboard sign under her arm and getting the plain dog for herself. Weeks later, Miss Gwendolyn started inviting her to come inside and sit with her.

They ate in silence at first. Then, out of the blue, Miss Gwendolyn started asking her questions. Was Answer Woman married, what did she do for a living, why did she eat her frankfurter plain. After telling paying customers they would come down with stage four inoperable melanoma that year, or that they'd lose their shirts in a certain mutual fund, Answer Woman found relief in these less grievous exchanges.

The day she met her brothers, Answer Woman sat with Miss Gwendolyn by her window. She couldn't imagine the old woman could see much past the glass, especially in the fading evening light. Miss Gwendolyn's hands shook as she clutched the tin foil around the hot dog, crushing the bun between her fingers. "Tell me about your childhood."

"Why do you want to know about that?"

"Is it such a strange thing to ask?" Miss Gwendolyn sighed. "I was reminiscing about my childhood today. I was the youngest of seven, if you can believe it, decrepit as I am now."

"I believe you."

"Any brothers or sisters?"

"Two brothers," Answer Woman said.

"Tell me about your home."

"What do you mean home?"

"Where you came from, genius."

From across the hall, a dog barked twice. A woman yelled back in a nasal Cantonese.

"I need you to ask me questions," Answer Woman said.

The old woman sighed again and coughed. "What was your neighborhood like?"

The answer tumbled from her lips, the way she'd expound on any question a customer had asked. "Postage-stamp gardens up and down the street. Our house was a small raised ranch. People called it the nice part of town, but it rested only a block or so away from the dodgy part, where we lived. The people who lived in the big house ran the glove factory." She could see the glove factory from the snow globe, magnified to life size, and saw a woman, pale eyes identical to her own, hair the same chestnut brown, the shape of her chin much the same as Edgar's. She clutched a picnic basket in front of her pregnant belly. She was young, and she was happy. Her hands smelled of coconut-based moisturizer her mother-in-law had given her two Christmases ago, a month after a Hawaiian vacation.

"Small towns with their small factories," Miss Gwendolyn said, shaking her head. "The factory closes and the whole town gets thrown out of work and then everyone's scraping to get by. That's why I moved to the city. Didn't want to end up like my sisters who stuck around, married deadbeats, waiting tables to make ends meet. I wanted to be a career woman."

"Do you keep in touch with your sisters?"

Miss Gwendolyn clicked her tongue. "Can't you see my bustling social life? Sisters and brothers and friends coming by every night of the week. And don't get me started on all of my boyfriends."

Answer Woman finished her hotdog and crumpled the foil into a little ball between her palms. "Nice talking with you."

Miss Gwendolyn stared out her window at a power line littered with streamers the past two weeks, the product of a party two floors above them, after which confetti and the shriveled remains of balloons had littered the sidewalk below.

"I'll see you tomorrow." After Answer Woman had left, she stood in the hallway until the last of the seven locks clicked into place.

#

Answer Woman shivered in the morning chill outside the museum. The street stunk, the air polluted with too many bodies and too much exhaust, the smells of a place that wasn't so much for the living as for the decaying. She waited for a customer amidst the columns of people who made their way past her sign. Few paused, much less stopped.

When Edgar arrived, he didn't hesitate to sit down on the museum steps beside his sister, while Butch paced the perimeter of the four squares of sidewalk closest to them. "The ability to answer these questions is a profound gift," Edgar said. "I'm sure you've recognized that?"

"Of course." The answer arrived automatically, but only partially true. Answer Woman recognized her power. She rarely considered it as a gift, though, so much as a set of unusual circumstances. Not so different from an unusually tall person who could reach the top shelf at the grocery store but had to endure cramped conditions on an airplane.

"When Butch and I were adopted together, we lived with a church-going family." Edgar reclined on the steps behind him and stretched. He extracted a circular tin from the pocket of his acid-washed dungarees and scooped a pinch of tobacco between this thumb and forefinger. The packaging was red, white, and blue and read Baseball Snuff. He offered the tin to her. She waved him off. "I'm trying to quit, myself," he said. "Ever since Butch there told me what would happen to my jaw and tongue if I kept it up." He plugged the tobacco between his lips and set to chewing. "Our new daddy was some ex-swamp preacher from Kentucky, and he told us whatever skills we had were a gift from the Lord. And what we did with them was our gift in return. Beautiful, right?"

Butch glided to his side for a pair of elongated steps before resuming his normal gait.

"When Butch recognized his ability, he asked himself questions about Jesus," Edgar said. "The answers rushed at him like riddles. Answers unlike any he gave in everyday conversation, answers in another voice altogether, if you get my drift."

"Not really," Answer Woman said.

"The thing is, Butch had started to reckon from what he knew to arrive at an absolute truth. He went to the community college library and studied up on physics and astronomy and quantum mechanics. He plumbed the depths of infinity." He tilted his head toward his brother. "He tried to figure out how the earth—how everything—is going to end one day. When all the stars burn out and the universe goes cold. All life vanishes everywhere. He went so far in his thinking and imagining that something snapped inside."

"And he explained all that to you?"

When Butch's orbit reached its nearest point to them, Edgar stood up and put a hand on his brother's shoulder. He guided him gently to a position at the bottom most step, where he hugged his knees beneath his chin and stared at the passersby.

"Not in so many words," Edgar said. "Bits and pieces. I think that other voice–the questions and riddles—is what he hears in his head now. He tried to talk to me more when he saw I knew the answers, too. Then I had the bright idea of trying again."

"Trying again?"

"Infinity and the end of the universe was too damn much for one man. We asked questions back and forth. Made progress, too. Answered questions. I had visions and felt feelings unlike anything I've felt before. Then I got dizzy. Then everything went black."

"It was still too much," Answer Woman said.

Edgar offered her a weak half-smile. "We began asking all manner of questions, and I lost all sense of time. I existed in those questions and answers. I woke up in a hospital bed, and after I put it together, I realized we'd been at it for five days straight— five days without food or water or sleep. We existed on ludes and cranberry juice. Whether the questions or the concentration or the exhaustion were the cause, my head ached for weeks afterward. And Butchie–he moved deeper and deeper into himself."

Butch pressed his fingertips into each other. His flat, bland face was expressionless.

"But now we have a third voice to spread the load, to speed the process. And a voice with keener abilities. A voice unaffected by the trials my brother endured, and more instinctually gifted than me." Edgar scratched a mole on his chin. "I've found buried treasures, slept with beautiful women, seen things I had no right to see. I've committed all manner of sins and gotten away with them. But do you know what I want to know?"

"You want to know everything," Answer Woman said.

Edgar lowered his lids flirtatiously and smiled at her again. "You, my lovely, are the missing link." Edgar reached out to touch her cheek. She slid away from him, and when he leaned after her, he clutched at his side the way he had before, muttering a curse under his breath.

"What happened to your ribs?"

"He touched the boxer's girlfriend here," Butch said, threading his hand between his legs.

Edgar glared at his brother and coughed violently. With an effort, he propped himself upright again and studied Answer Woman. "It's nothing for you to be concerned about. It's time you stopped whoring out your powers and come back to our place so we can work."

Answer Woman planted her feet. "That's a bad idea."

"Why? Because you need to make money to buy bratwurst for Miss Gwendolyn?" Edgar smiled, the spaces between his teeth wet with tobacco juice. He started to reach for her again, but stopped himself and reached for his brother instead, scratching him behind the ear the way he would a puppy. Butch dipped into the touch. "You're our sister, and we care about you. We'll give you another day to digest what we talked about."

"You'll give me one more day and then what?"

"One more day and you'll make the right decision," Edgar said.

He handed her a scrap of paper, the size of a business card, but on taking it, she realized the material had been ripped from a napkin. The address for an apartment in the old meatpacking district. When Answer Woman peered back up to her brothers, they were already walking away.

#

Walking home, Answer Woman threw out the address Edgar had given her. She contemplated a new spot to peddle her answers the next day. But if Edgar wanted to find her, all he would need to do was ask Butch where she had gone.

To her surprise, her brothers never arrived. She had a good day on the steps, fielding seven customers, one of whom tipped her an extra twenty when she gave him the good news that his pregnant wife was carrying his child, and not her former lover's.

She climbed the steps of her apartment building, plain hotdog in her left hand, the one with sauerkraut and relish in the right. When she set foot on the mildewed green carpet of her floor, she heard the first bark of the neighbor's dog and caught the first whiff of grilled pineapple from the first door by the stairwell. The door to Miss Gwendolyn's apartment was cracked open.

She never left her door ajar, even when she expected company. Answer Woman dropped both hotdogs and ran.

Miss Gwendolyn lay on the floor, eyes open, a hand on her chest. Gathering herself, Answer Woman dropped to the ground and started chest compressions.

"Is she dead?"

Answer Woman recognized the voice. She blinked away tears as the answer came to her.

Edgar stood in the doorway. He took a bite of the hotdog meant for Miss Gwendolyn. "We figured the best chance someone would find her was to leave the door open."

"You should have called 911 for help."

"We don't have a phone." Edgar leaned against the door. On the door frame opposite him, the connecting halves of seven locks waited.

"How did you get inside? She didn't know you. She never would have let you in."

Edgar pursed his lips, but Butch spoke up from behind him. "The window."

The window was wide open, the screen on the floor by the radiator. "Did you kill her?"

Edgar shook his head from side-to-side.

"Yes," Butch volunteered, a beat behind him.

"Shades of gray." Edgar said. "We came to the window to talk to her. Guess we scared her, and she must've stroked out. I swear, I kicked in the screen to help her. But when I asked Butch if she was already gone—he told me the same thing you did."

Answer Woman held Miss Gwendolyn's hand. "Why would you come to her?"

"I thought you'd listen to her," Edgar said. "Butchie tells me you don't have other friends. I figured maybe the old bag could help you see you shouldn't turn away family."

Answer Woman let herself sob. "You pricks want to use me."

"Can't you see you were meant for this?" Edgar asked. "I'm not using you any more than I'm using Butch, or than he's using me. We're going to work together, and we're going to figure out everything. Once we know it all, we'll have accomplished something. We can be happy."

"That will make you happy?"

"Fucking-A, yes," Edgar said.

"No," Butch said.

Edgar elbowed his brother aside. "What do you say we go to your place and get to work?"

A minute later, Answer Woman sat on her ottoman with the worn velvet lining, directly beneath the crack in her ceiling she'd always feared would give way and send her neighbor's living room crashing into her own. Sinking into the cushion of her best chair, Edgar sat cross-legged, white Keds browned from the streets folded beneath him. Swiveling from side-to-side. Butch sat on a bar stool Answer Woman had taken home from a street corner years ago.

When Butch hummed, Answer Woman caught the melody this time. Recalled the lyrics.

Sing it loud so I can hear you.

Make it easy to be near you.

She lost the words after that.

"How about a cup of Joe?" Edgar asked.

"I don't have any."

Edgar rolled his eyes. "Then what about a glass of milk, or V-8?"

She went into her kitchen and filled an unwashed glass with tap water.

Edgar didn't look twice at the violet tint of the water. He gulped the water in one long swallow. "Are we ready?" Edgar explained what they would do in greater detail. Through questions, they would travel backwards in time. They would do it in measured steps—asking what came before a certain moment, then what came before that. They would go backward rather than forward since the future held too many variables, might require too much calculation.

"What came before us?" Edgar asked.

"Our mother," Butch said.

Answer Woman felt her throat stick at the words.

"An un-ambitious start." Edgar scraped his fingernail against the bottom of the tin of chewing tobacco, groping for the final bits. "Go on, ask me."

She was supposed to ask him what came before their mother. "Is our mother still alive?"

Edgar sounded annoyed. "That's irrelevant."

Answer Woman turned to Butch. "Is our mother still alive?"

"Yes."

"We need to fucking focus." Edgar rocked in his chair.

"Where is she now—our mother?"

"Gravesend Mental Hospital." Butch said. "Thirty-nine-forty-two Chestnut Way, Shermantown, New York. Room two-forty-seven."

Answer Woman bolted from her ottoman.

Edgar yelled at her to stop. He took a step forward, then tripped over Butch's legs. Butch fell off the stool, half beneath his brother, half on top of him, and howling in pain.

Answer Woman ran to her bedroom

"We need to finish this." Edgar knelt by Butch.

She snatched at her money, ripping the bills from their hiding place in the slit of her mattress. She bundled a couple thousand dollars in cash and stuffed it inside a backpack with frayed white ropes for straps. She placed two fresh pairs of underpants, socks, and a clean blouse on top of the money, and zipped shut the bag. She headed for the door.

Edgar moved much faster than she had seen him move before. He tackled her, then straddled her. He gripped her wrists and pinned her to the floor. "We aren't done with you."

Answer Woman fought. She planted her feet and pushed upward, bridging herself. Edgar budged at first, then he flattened himself, chest to chest, thighs on thighs, his face inches above hers. Tobacco flecked the cracks between his stained teeth. He swept her hair back, pulled it to the floor behind her ear. "How about a kiss, darling?"

He had loosened her left hand. She jammed it into his ribcage with as much force as she could muster and dug her knuckles into the space between two ribs. He rolled off of her.

Answer Woman ran. She felt the rush of the snow globe before it exploded against the door. Broken glass, water, and tiny buildings littered the linoleum.

Now on his knees, Edgar screamed, "You walk out on us, and you'd better pray you never see us again. You walk out on us, and I'll end you. Go ahead, ask me if I'm lying."

#

Over time, Answer Woman had learned bits of her past. She hitchhiked after she left her adoptive parents. One driver slowed his truck, leaned down and asked her, "Where's your daddy?"

"Some of him is buried in my mother's yard," she said.

Another time, at a coffee shop on St. Mark's Place, in the East Village, two hack writers debated whether their screenplay should have the father threaten his daughter with his belt or a broken bottle. They contested which was more frightening, which more painful.

"The belt's scarier," she told them. "But the cuts from the glass take longer to heal."

After she left her brothers behind at her apartment, Answer Woman took a cab to the Port Authority. Her brothers would know where to find her, and she wasn't ready to take Edgar at his word that he didn't want to see her again. If she got a head start and put some distance between them, maybe she could tend to more important matters first.

She boarded a bus headed north and took a window seat toward the back. One of the last passengers to get on the bus was a broad-shouldered man in a red-gray beard and black and gold checkered flannel shirt, the sleeves rolled up to the elbows. Answer Woman recognized him, a poker buddy of the man she had dated who came from Shermantown. Lowering her face, Answer Woman drew the drawstrings on her hooded sweatshirt tight. She meant to sleep through the journey, but the other passengers asked questions she could hear.

A bald man in a brown suede jacket asked a girl with tawny skin and pink-framed glasses where she was headed.

Home, to break up with her meth dealing boyfriend, so she can stop feeling guilty about going down on her econ professor.

"Why are you scratching your head?"

He has lice.

"How long till we get there?"

Eight hours, thirty-five minutes.

"Did you drink this morning?"

Two shots of tequila and a mouthful of Listerine so you wouldn't smell it.

People started watching Answer Woman. She had only thought the answers, hadn't she? She pulled up the hood of her sweatshirt and pulled the drawstrings taut to cover her mouth.

The bus parked at a rest stop. She bought a pair of headphones and a portable radio, then listened to a classical music station at full volume for the rest of the ride.

When she got off the bus for good, a wintry wind greeted her. Someone called her name.

The poker buddy had spotted her. In the same easy fashion of her ex-boyfriend, he transitioned effortlessly from salutation to conversation, and with the same belabored vowel sounds. "I had to come home because my ma's sick. I begged her to come see a specialist in the City, but she insists on her country doc because the geezer lets her pay her bills in lima beans and squash from her garden in the summer." He shook his head.

"Which way is Gravesend?" Answer Woman asked.

"The looney bin?" The man stretched his hairy forearm behind her. "Top of the hill."

She left him standing there without another word, heading for what a building atop a hill, something like a gothic mansion. In the fading daylight, she walked two miles at an incline. The air felt different in Shermantown than it had in New York. Easier to breathe. She passed the red brick schoolhouse, unchanged from what the snow globe had modeled. She passed the factory, its windows boarded up with plywood. A large sign–what probably passed for a billboard in a town like this–advertising Rose Cakes. They were chocolate, it turned out, with neon pink frosting. The last quarter mile, the road turned to cobblestone. She climbed until she arrived at Gravesend.

In the softly lit lobby, Answer Woman folded her hands on the counter, took a deep breath, and said, "I came to see my mother."

The freckled man on the other side of the counter positioned his fingers over a computer keyboard, covered in protective plastic. "What's her name?" His own nametag read Nelson.

"Abigail Wolfe." The syllables felt strange on her tongue, the first time she had spoken them.

The psychiatric hospital wasn't as clean and sterile as Answer Woman had expected it to be. In place of waxed tile floors and bare white walls, they walked over scratched hardwood and passed paint-by-number seascapes over peeling orange-and-white-striped wallpaper.

"We don't want Gravesend to feel like an institution," Nelson explained. "We find the patients feel more comfortable if the place feels more like a home. We let them decorate and keep their personal things. As much as they can fit into their rooms anyway."

From the other side of the door at room two-forty-seven, Answer Woman could hear a guitar, soft and low. Nelson knocked but didn't wait for a response.

An elderly woman faced out a window, perfectly still in a caned rocking chair. Her uncombed hair was gray-streaked, and her wrinkled skin sagged on her neck. Her hands rested open on her lap to reveal thick scars on both palms.

A record player spun in the corner. Answer Woman recognized the song, one she hadn't heard for years. But she knew the melody and had heard pieces of it in wordless hums.

> *Who knows how long I've loved you?*
> *You know I love you still.*
> *Will I wait a lonely lifetime?*

Answer Woman stepped inside. "If you want me to, I will."

"She loves her music." Nelson stood sideways in the door. "Mostly Beatles, a little Dylan, some Judy Collins. If you catch her on a good day, she'll talk about them."

Answer Woman stared out the window. Nothing but the dark blue eastern sky. Nelson retreated from the doorway, the jangle of his keys receding down the hall.

"Where am I?" the old woman asked.

Answer Woman recoiled. The old woman had startled her by speaking at all.

The old woman's eyes remained fixed on the sapphire sky. "Who are you?"

Answer Woman searched for signs of familiarity, for features of the old woman, mirrored between them. "I don't know."

The old woman blinked rapidly. "What time is it?"

Answer Woman scanned the walls. A navy-blue tapestry hung over one. Holes pockmarked the next, left over from long-gone nails and pushpins, cracked with the collisions of humanity against plaster. She couldn't find a clock. "I don't know."

"Why are we here?"

Hot tears rolled down Answer Woman's cheeks, bubbling over like a broth left to boil too long, the pot too full. She couldn't answer. She knelt at the old woman's feet and kissed the scars on her mother's hands.

Understand

They parked on the outskirts of the ghost town, Old Dunberry, a place Mona had told Eleanor was special to her family. So special they all wound up there for reunions, funeral, weddings.

"We're the first to arrive," Eleanor said, observing the absence of other cars and the way the dust kicked up from beneath the tires of Mona's Volkswagen as if it were rousing specks of the dead, because no one else had driven into this dirt for hours, maybe day.

"We're not the first." Mona threaded an arm through Eleanor's and grasped her hand. Her skin was smooth and cool to the touch. She carried the scent of rose petals and cinnamon. "Come on."

Mona wore a striking red dress that felt both too modern and too bright for the dusty desert setting. Eleanor had dressed more conservatively in a plain black dress that covered her shoulders and reached past her knees. She'd learned even families that professed to be fine with a same-sex couple would have their outliers who weren't and who'd pick up on any detail they might criticize as evidence this relationship wasn't up to code. Better to have the most judgmental of them think she was a prude than a slut.

Mona carried the envelope with the card for the relatives distant enough she'd had to double-check the spelling of the names, and Eleanor certainly couldn't remember them. Mona'd made out the card from them both, though Eleanor had protested it should be from Mona alone. Let her take the credit. After all, it was her family. Mona disagreed. She said family was an ocean. Trace it back far enough and who could distinguish one sea from another, which drop of water could be attributed to which storm. Go back far enough and everybody was intertwined through time and space.

Eleanor told her she liked that, and Mona said to be prepared because her family talked about big ideas and metaphors. They loved stories most of all and Eleanor should have some at the ready. They could be stories from Eleanor's family or stories she'd made up, but they could also be stories she'd heard, stories she read, because in the end, who could own a story?

"I understand," Eleanor said.

They walked through the threshold together, under the old wooden sign with *WELCOME TO OLD DUNBERRY* carved into the face of it, supported by a rickety wooden post on either side. Not a soul in sight, Eleanor asked where they'd go first.

"Feel like a drink?" Mona asked.

Of course Eleanor did, because though she didn't drink much, so much of her relationship with Mona had centered on drinking from their first date at a bar to the cocktails Mona mixed in her kitchen to sip while they watched true crime documentaries after dark. Meeting Mona's family—that was an occasion for drink, for sure, to celebrate, to calm her nerves, to be the better version of herself Mona and alcohol seemed to extract by equal measures.

Whereas the welcome sign at the edge of the ghost town had appeared unstable, the bar's signage—reading *Saloon* in the plainest of sans-serif print—had fallen altogether, on-the-ground and dusty. They walked right through the door, the whole ghost town open for them to explore, and Eleanor remembered visiting places like this is a child and being instructed to express wonder at butter churns and printing presses. All the most boring things. But if Old Dunberry meant something to Mona, it would mean something to Eleanor, too, even if it meant swallowing her disappointment at not having an actual drink to imbibe but rather raising dusty old tumblers to pantomime drinking, a form of play. She imagined that's about what she was up against in this relic of a bar. It couldn't possibly have anything potable inside.

But inside, Eleanor did spot her first soul, seated at the bar. She was a hunch-backed old woman with surprisingly broad shoulders. Mona rushed to her and hugged her awfully hard for such a brittle old timer.

Mona introduced Eleanor as her girlfriend, making no apologies or deflections about it, which felt good. The woman hugged Eleanor, too, firmer than she would have expected, and Mona explained she was her grandmother, Esmerelda.

"Call me Esme," she corrected her. Her eyes seemed to glitter a silvery blue. She asked Eleanor if she wanted a drink.

Esme got off her stool with a bit of effort, shunning Mona's outstretched hand to help her, and teetered to the far side of the bar, where she found two glass tumblers and a crystalline bottle, refracting rainbows out of light Eleanor hadn't noticed shining in the first place. The old woman poured the whiskey straight while Eleanor tried to wrap her head around the mechanics of the situation—if Mona's family brought their own provisions when they visited the ghost town, or worked out an arrangement with the owners when they'd be in town, or if the whole arrangement were illicit, and Esme was simply too old to care about rules and helped herself to what she could find in Old Dunberry.

They sat at a high table on teetering stools. Mona coiled an ankle around Eleanor's and stroked her skin a couple times before resting, legs knotted up out of sight. The whiskey was strong, but smooth. Too easy to drink, and though Esme poured her another shot without asking, Eleanor cradled the glass, waiting to sip until the first drink had caught up to her and she could gauge how drunk she was.

Once an extended exchange of pleasantries was out of the way, Esme got to what Mona had warned her about. "Tell me a story."

And Eleanor had one at the ready. One befitting a ghost town, one she'd read in a magazine sometime before about a company that rented ghosts to its customers a year at a time. Esme chuckled at the concept. So, Eleanor went on, trying to not to be too performative, trying not to sound rehearsed.

She spoke about a man renting ghosts, always intending to catch up with an old lover, but she was never available to him, until finally she was. But nothing came across like he expected it to when he had her in his home because she felt like he was holding her captive, and all he wanted was to hear her sing.

Esme turned the bottom of her glass up to down a mighty gulp of her whiskey at the end of the story, then set down the tumbler hard against the table. "An excellent story," she said. "People think time and death can change how people feel. But time's all an illusion. It's all happening at once. Close your eyes tight enough, long enough, and remember a time long ago. You're there, back in the moment. No wiser, not better for all this time, time, time."

"I understand," Eleanor said, though she wasn't sure she understood altogether. But she understood the story had made a good impression. She understood the hand she felt rubbing her shoulder to be Mona's, and Mona was impressed with how she'd carried herself. That meant something.

#

Eleanor met the twin brothers at the town bank. Curtis and Nick took turns adding coins to an old-timey balance scale in what seemed like a competition as to who could make the scale tip all the way down to his side first. Neither were Mona's blood relatives, both married into the family via different cousins. One met his wife at the other's wedding, and it all felt a little incestuous. "But trace it back far enough, and aren't we all family?" Nick said.

The truth was, the duo came across as boyish at the scale, giggling at one another as they placed their coins at different speeds and with different degrees of severity, ultimately debating then and there whether one was allowed to throw a coin down and what constituted a throw vs. a lob, and from what height a drop or flip of a coin became a throw. They were men in their twenties, younger than Eleanor and Mona, but not by much.

Men who certainly should have outgrown arguments this idiosyncratic, but then Eleanor recalled how old jealousies she'd long come to peace with bubbled back to the surface over Christmas dinner with her sister. The drive to fall back on old habits, on default modes of relationships had to be stronger among twins, and probably among boys who never outgrew games in the first place.

"You like Old Dunberry so far?" Nick asked. Nick with the moustache. Nick in the black shirt to Curtis's white. Eleanor imagined they might have coordinated such details to differentiate themselves when they'd be in the same space at the same time, though she also remembered Mona telling her about their trickster side—a propensity to trade baseball caps or t-shirts in their youth for the express purpose of confusing everyone as to who was who.

"It's nice." Eleanor stayed noncommittal, because while nice or a *nicer* answer would've been suitable fodder for Esme or one of Mona's parents, the brothers might have been poking fun at her. Mona had warned about that, too.

"A nice place to collect dust," Curtis said. "Some place to bring a date, Mona. Going to bring her by the American quilting museum next?"

Mona planted a hand to the small of Eleanor's back, leaned forward, and rested a thumb on the edge of Nick's side of the scale, awarding him the victory—tainted as it may be—but more to the point ruining the game. They must have expected it, though, because they hardly complained, instead offering their fuller attention as they asked Eleanor where she was from and about her family. Curtis asked if Mona still snored at night and offered a startlingly good impression of what her snore really did sound like—a soft guttural sucking, a wisp of an exhale.

Nick locked eyes with Eleanor and asked if she had a story to tell them.

Eleanor told them a story about a time when all the dogs had died out from the world. Except one, who showed up, unceremoniously, unassumingly, at the doorstep of a man whose wife had a left him, a man desperate to use the dog to court favor with the daughter they split custody of, but in the back of his mind, more importantly, imagining this dog might bring the family back together.

"What happened?" Curtis asked.

"The dog died," Eleanor said. "The wife remarried."

"A real heartbreaker." Nick smiled and haphazardly swept the coins off his side of the scale, then Curtis's, resetting for the next game.

A girl rushed by, maybe seven or eight years old, between where the brothers played at the scale and where Eleanor and Mona stood. Eleanor remembered visiting museums as a child. The eternal paradox that they were at once places of wonder for a child to look at mysterious things but also spaces not to run or climb for fear of breaking something ancient.

Curtis was on it, though, snatching up the girl by her waist. She giggled, familiar. "Speaking of heartbreakers, here's one in the making."

The girl laughed in a feral way at getting lifted mid-stride.

Nick winked at her. "Esme, what'd we tell you about running around in here—especially when we have visitors?"

Esme's eyes were a bright blue at the edge of silver there in the bank. Her eyes were game for mischief, as hungry for stories as anyone Eleanor was likely to meet.

"I understand," she said.

#

Eleanor was feeling hazy when Mona wrapped an arm around her waist and offered her the water canteen. Eleanor apologized, realizing her fatigue must have shown in her loping, staggering gait, and Mona waved her off saying no mere mortal should try to match Grandma Esme drink for drink.

Mona supported Eleanor, locked hip to hip like conjoined sisters. "I should warn you, my aunt is eccentric. She lost her mind after the murder."

Eleanor had questions of course, but before she could get out the words about the aunt or the murder, they were upon her. Mona exclaimed *Aunt Clarice!* and hugged the woman tightly.

Aunt Clarice didn't hesitate to hug Eleanor before any introductions. "I've missed you," Clarice said in a way Eleanor might have read as flirtatious, even seductive under other circumstances than a family function, meeting her niece's girlfriend.

"This is the first time you've met Eleanor," Mona said, her voice rigid in the manner of strong-arming a child into saying the right nicety.

"Of course, of course, of course." Clarice's voice diminished on every repetition to the point of whispering the last one. Her body shrank inward, too, like a cat coiling, readying herself to pounce. "How do you like Old Dunberry so far?"

"It's quaint." Eleanor wasn't sure that was the right word. *Quaint* might sound condescending to a place so important to their family. Wasn't there something about a place people had ownership over, attachments to—a place they called home? That very particular mix of pride and shame, that sense they were free to poke fun at it but no one else could dare.

"Quaint, quaint, quaint." Clarice smiled. She was quite young, to the point Eleanor would have guessed she was Mona's sister or cousin. Probably an aunt on a technicality, one of the youngest of the preceding generation, Mona one of the eldest. "I suppose city girls find anything outside the city limits quaint?"

Eleanor started to explain she didn't mean any disrespect, and Mona talked over her to ask about the weather this past year, when another woman arrived quite suddenly and locked Clarice into a tackling embrace. They had a strong resemblance between them. This new arrival wore a long, sleeveless dress, black with a floral print over it.

The women giggled, almost losing their balance. It must have been ages since they'd seen each other, but wasn't that the spirit of a wedding, to bring family together across distances and time? Clarice closed her eyes tight and gave the woman a squeeze. When she opened her eyes, she asked. "Have you met Esmerelda?"

"We've run into Esme," Mona said. "Or I should say she's run into us."

"Don't go shortening my name." She had a hint of a southern lilt to her voice, maybe put on, or maybe because she'd relocated somewhere southerly and taken it on by degrees.

She locked eyes with Eleanor, undeniably a beautiful woman. The word *heartbreaker* the brothers had used came back to Eleanor's mind. The kind of woman who'd set sights on who she wanted and pursue them shamelessly, if only because she knew she'd get what she wanted in the end. Mona was like that, too. Mona'd made the first move on their first date, before Eleanor was certain she was on a date, and explained later that she didn't see any point in subtlety. Mona wanted everything she had coming to her.

"It's Esmerelda." The woman elongated every syllable. "Savor the flavor."

"Take it easy, Grandma, she's mine." Mona kissed Eleanor, soft with a little tongue. "Clarice, why don't you tell Eleanor about the man you killed?"

Clarice did tell the tale, heavy on facts, light on narrative, about a husband who drank and knocked her around and that was all right enough, except then he knocked around her son from a previous marriage, too, so she rigged a shelf full of paint cans to fall on her husband's head when he was working in the garage. The state brought her to trial, but no one could prove she was responsible.

"I'm impressed you'd share that all with me," Eleanor said. "We just met." She regretted saying it once the words were out because it felt like it would invite a follow-up threat about keeping her mouth shut.

"The story's from a long time ago," Clarice said.

Next thing, Eleanor was telling her next story, someplace between distracting from tensions and appeasement, and settling into a groove of telling the stories she knew, the stranger the better because this family enjoyed magic and metaphor.

"This is a story about a boy made out of stone whose friend fell in love with a girl made of glass."

"Sounds fragile," Esmerelda said. "I bet she broke."

"She did," Eleanor said. "But I haven't told you about the boy made of fire yet."

Esmerelda and Clarice listened; their eyes were aglow.

#

"I should explain about Esme," Mona said.

"I understand," Eleanor said. "She explained it from the start. About time."

Mona watched her closely. An intense look like the lazy Sunday afternoon in Eleanor's kitchen when a peach-strawberry pie browned in the oven and the dishes piled up in the sink and Mona hugged her tight and asked her if she'd come to meet her family in Old Dunberry—if she'd come to a wedding.

Some questions carried more weight than others. No space for questions in return or hesitation if she didn't want to risk Mona skittering away. Eleanor said yes.

"You understand," Mona said.

#

Eleanor met Mona's parents—the meeting she'd feared most, because in her experience every time she met a significant other's parents was awkward. But whether they were disinterested in uncomfortable encounters or distracted by the nuptials about to begin they didn't ask her questions and didn't insist on a story. Mona's father was austere, but not unkind. He wore a tuxedo with tails. Mona's mother was warmer. She said, "Welcome to the family."

The wedding took place on a wooden stage at the center of Old Dunberry, rows of wooden folding chairs set out before it.

A perfect faith rain wouldn't come, the sun wouldn't beat down too hot and bright. Eleanor could imagine this stage's use in times past. A space for the mayor to make proclamations to all the townsfolk. A spot for public punishment—reprobates in stocks, people hanged. Under those circumstances, the natural elements would only enhance the suffering.

But that day, the stage was the setting for a wedding, with ropes of pastel flowers, hung in uneven loops. Eleanor found something refreshing in them not being perfectly aligned. She imagined someone from the family had wrangled them, maybe children. A string band played folksy, wordless tunes, the guitar out of tune, the stand-up bass player taking liberties with his raucous pizzicato, threatening to drown out the fiddle's melody.

Eleanor didn't get a good look at the groom, only saw he wore a tuxedo a lot like Mona's dad, and his hair was so thoroughly slicked back it appeared almost plastic. Little Esme was a flower girl, in a dress with flowers a lot like the ones used to decorate the stage, all soft pinks and violets. Squint your eyes and the flowers turned to clouds, to a sunset.

The bride was a dead ringer for Mona. She wore a strapless white dress with a flowing, gossamer skirt. When she took the groom's hand, Mona took Eleanor's, too, interlacing fingers, giving a squeeze.

The ceremony was short, to the point. Barely enough to feel like an occasion. The officiant—she looked like old Esme—told a story about a man whose friend was made of stone, whose love was made of glass.

Mona held Eleanor's hand tighter.

When the groom lifted back the veil for a kiss, all Eleanor could see was Mona's face. Eleanor and Mona were on stage. Esme proclaimed they may kiss. The touched noses. Smelling of makeup. A little of lilac. Mona moved in to close the distance between their lips. Eleanor met her tongue with hers, just a touch like slapping five, like a stolen look.

Esme pronounced them brides.

At the reception, Eleanor took her turn holding baby Esme, rocking her in her arms, cooing. She told her a story about a woman who knew the answers to every question, about how quickly a gift could become a burden. About how a burden could be overcome, redeemed, made into something new or very old. It was all the same.

Esme settled.

The mother took the baby back. Mona took Eleanor by the hand to lead her to the center of the reception—the dirt dance floor left behind after a collective effort to remove all the chairs from the ceremony. Nick sent Clarice twirling by her fingertips. Curtis dipped the sultriest version of Esme. She led his hand to where her skirt shrank back, to her bare thigh.

Mona and Eleanor swayed as the band played a song Eleanor didn't recognize by name but recognized as theirs. A song she'd heard a million times, but softer and slower now.

"Tell me a story," Mona whispered in her ear.

Eleanor began to tell her about a world without dogs and a man grieving his marriage. She stopped herself. "I'm sorry. I've told you this one before."

"Every story's been told," Mona said. "I've heard every one." She was stunning. Hair curled ever so slightly, face bright, attracting every light in the town square so she shone, radiant. Or maybe Eleanor had it flipped. Maybe Mona she was light enough to illuminate everything around her, the light not drawn to, but projected from her. She did feel hot to the touch. She did smell like summer and flowers and an ocean and forever.

"The difference is in the telling," Mona said. "The details you notice. The turn of phrase. Do you understand?"

Eleanor lifted a hand to brush back Mona's hair. Any excuse to touch. She started from the beginning again.

Worlds Away

I read a lot of science fiction, and truth be told spent a lot of my waking time daydreaming about worlds impossibly far away.

My father didn't share any of that with me. He kept a loaded Remington in the gun cabinet he never locked. I had fired the gun a couple dozen times on the range. Three times in the woods. All misses, aimed at a doe, when my father and his friends decided to take their almost-teenaged sons hunting. My father snapped at me to stop shooting or I'd scare away the rest of the goddamned deer.

We lived on the edge of Shermantown, New York, in a one-story, two-bedroom home painted forest green in two different chipped shades. I remember it was spring, but the temperatures still didn't reach past the mid-forties.

My mother was working the swing shift at Fat Lenny's then, and one night my little sister Maggie and I had tried to make spaghetti. We called to ask what qualified as a rolling boil and again to ask how soft the noodles should get. Mom told us her boss didn't appreciate her talking on the phone when she was supposed to be waiting tables and warned us never to call her at work again. If we needed anything, we should talk to Dad.

The trouble was most nights Dad didn't stick around. Occasionally, he'd sit in the living room and drink through a baseball game on our seventeen-inch Sony television. More often, he drank his whiskey straight with the deadbeats and drifters at the tavern around the corner.

After we'd finished our microwave dinners, I insisted Maggie and I hang out in the dark. The television was easier to watch without the reflection of the standup lamp in the living room. The narrow glow of a flashlight made it easier to disappear into the worlds of pulp science fiction books—books I used to shoplift from the rack by the door at Mahanna's. Darkness made it easier, too, to beat a hasty retreat when the headlights of our mother's station wagon shone through the front window, or at the sound of our father's footsteps leading up to the doorway. We'd spring into our bedroom, duck under the covers, and act as though we'd turned in by our ten o'clock bedtime.

That night, I'd finished a new book about an alien invasion with an unhappy ending; I intended to tuck it under my bed and remove a better book to reread— *War of the Worlds.*

Dad never let us raise the thermostat past fifty-five degrees, but as I walked into the bedroom, it seemed colder than usual. I felt the breeze before I spotted the open window or the head poking through it. Curly black hair, a round swollen face. A puffy red winter coat.

His upper body was well inside the window frame, but it seemed he was stuck. He curled his tongue over his upper lip.

I barked.

I wasn't particularly bright or athletic or funny, but in those days my claim to fame was my ability to authentically imitate the bark, howl, and panting sounds of a large, angry dog. The jocks frequently deployed me to terrorize smaller boys who couldn't see us coming, their faces buried in their lockers. In lieu of any other obvious talent, I made dog sounds when we visited family at Christmas time, too. Maggie played violin.

I crouched in the shadows so the man at the window wouldn't see me, and I gave my harshest slobbering dog sounds. The man froze. His foot slipped from its tenuous perch on the sill. He scrambled backward. Heavy footsteps. Ragged breath. He was gone.

I waited there a minute on the floor, then ran to the window, slammed it down, turned the lock and drew shut the ratty brown curtains, all in trembling, clumsy motions.

Back in the living room, Maggie was oblivious. She wouldn't have thought anything of the sound of me practicing my bark. My sister sat cross legged, her face six inches from the television on mute—I couldn't read with the noise—while images of cop cars with flashing lights crossed the screen, bathing the room in the sickly blue light of a show I probably should have stopped an eight-year-old from watching. I considered telling her what had happened but scaring her wouldn't do either of us any good. Our house was under siege—only a matter of time before the would-be burglar or abductor or murderer or rapist might figure out what had happened and double back. Maybe with reinforcements.

I turned to the recliner. An empty bottle of Jim Beam was tipped on its side, a wasted drop drying into a brown stain on the beige polyester where the mouth of the bottle hung over the seat. Beside it, a thread-worn copy of *A Farewell to Arms*.

I decided to make the call. I found a tavern matchbook in the kitchen junk drawer, stretched the telephone cord from its hall-cradle into our bedroom, and pushed the door most of the way shut. That way, I reasoned, Maggie wouldn't hear me, but I'd be able to hear if the man returned to the house through a different entry.

The phone rang fourteen times without an answer. I hung up and pressed the numbers on the keypad again. After four more rings, a voice scratched across the line: "Yeah?"

I swallowed. The spit hung in my throat for a second and I gagged. "Can I please speak to Jerry Kip?"

A long exhale, then I didn't hear anything. He might have hung up. But then the cry came out, loud enough to hurt my ear: "Kip!"

I waited. No voices, but no dial tone either. No clatter of the fat man kicking down the front door or the sound of a saw cutting through the back screen. No smash of the living room window. The whole world was on mute.

My father answered the phone the way he did at home. "This is Kip."

"Dad, it's Jacob," I said. "Some guy tried to get in the house."

I waited. He'd be angry at the man in the window, but he'd have no one to target but me. He would ask *what happened?* and *did the bastard take anything?* and *did the sonufabitch lay a finger on Maggie?* All the things fathers in books said.

But he questions never came.

So, I went on. "He already had the window open when I came in. He was trying to climb through, so I barked like a dog." Pride swelled in me. "And he ran away."

My father exhaled into the phone in a long unsteady stream. I could all but smell the whiskey through the line. "You calling to brag?"

A bright white light shone through the curtain and lit the bedroom for a second. It disappeared. Just a passing car. "No, Dad," I said. "I was scared. I thought maybe you could come home."

"Scared." My father tried on the word. "What are you scared of?"

Glass rattled from beyond the bedroom. My pulse pounded. I put my hand back on the cold metal doorknob. The glass rattled again, followed by a light thud. I recognized it as the sound of Maggie opening and closing the refrigerator—the pickle and mayonnaise jars and the glass bottle of Heinz all shaking from their compartment in the door.

"Speak up." His voice had taken on an edge.

"I'm scared he'll come back." I felt a familiar stickiness in the back of my throat. I swallowed hard to force it back down and ran my sweater sleeve over my eyes to make sure they stayed dry.

"Remember when I took you hunting?" Dad asked. "Remember how to shoot?"

I didn't say yes, but rather an *mmm* sound. The best I could manage without a sob.

"Then why are you calling me?"

My father hung up. I waited with the receiver to my ear for a few seconds longer.

By now, Maggie had resumed her post by the television, seated sideways, knees bent, feet kicked back so her heels almost touched her butt. She scooped chocolate and vanilla swirled pudding from a plastic container small enough to fit in the palm of her hand and ran her lip over the top of the spoonful, eating

138

the pudding layer by layer, a string of saliva connecting her lips to her dessert each time she withdrew.

"Don't sit like that," I said. "It's bad for your hip."

She shifted without comment, so her legs were stretched straight out in front of her, white socks with blue and yellow and pink stars touching the TV stand, her big toe poking through a hole in the left one.

I scooped up the plaid quilt I'd worn earlier, still molded to fit my body, and draped it over my shoulder before I crossed behind Maggie to the gun cabinet in the corner—really just an old oak dresser, repurposed when Mom told Dad he needed to keep his firearms someplace out of sight, or she'd always be nervous about them. The cabinet hinges squealed when they opened. Maggie still had her eyes fixed on the screen.

The rifle waited inside and for the first time indoors, I lifted it in my hands. *That's eight pounds of life and death*, my father had told me in the woods. *Aim careful. Shoot clean.* I ran a thumb over the safety and elected to keep it in place. I figured if the fat man came back, I could release it first. One last warning.

In the meantime, I wrapped the rifle in the blanket to keep it hidden from Maggie. After I sat back down on the couch, I remembered the book I'd gotten up for. On the television, a squat man in a khaki police uniform had his gun drawn. He saved the day in a silent world, impossibly far away.

Acknowledgments

My deepest gratitude to Juan Martinez, Jennifer Harris, and the team at JackLeg Press for believing in this collection and ushering it into the world.

Versions of some work in this collection were originally published elsewhere as follows: "This Year's Ghost" in *The Pinch*, "Dog Days" in *The Heavy Feather Review*, "Stone" in *Hot Metal Bridge*, "Clown Faces" in *Things You Can Create* and *Circus Folk*, fragments from "Reel-to-Reel" in *Shirley Magazine* and *Dream Journal*, "Bet Your Life!" in *Big Muddy*, "Take Me Home" in *The Non-Binary Review*, "Answer Woman" in *The Normal School*, "Understand" in *Miniskirt Magazine*, and "Worlds Away" in *BULL*. A special thanks to Jared Duran, Janell Hughes, and Hoot n Waddle Press for their enthusiasm and encouragement around my offbeat stories about clowns and circuses.

Thank you to the writing communities at Oregon State and Johns Hopkins. Profound thanks to my mentors, including Marjorie Sandor, Nick Dybek, Susan Jackson Rodgers, Keith Scribner, Harvey Grossinger, and Elly Williams, who remain voices in my ear each time I write and whom each weighed in directly on at least one story in this collection. My gratitude to Ben Davis, Dylan Brown, Gretchen Schrafft, Ian Sacks, Julia Malye, Lacey Rowland, Mackenzie Evan Smith, Meg Goss, Sam Mitchell, Sarah Kosch, and TJ Neathery for your input on a range of pieces herein.

Thank you to Jason Teal, Jennifer A. Howard, and Tara Kerr Roberts for your generous support of this book.

I'm indebted to my friends, colleagues, and students from the UNLV Honors College, Georgia Gwinnett College, and the Center for Talented Youth. My work with you informed aspects of this collection, big and small, from the first inklings of its first stories to the point at which the book, at last, took shape.

Thanks to my family and friends. Specifically, to Mike Scalise, Mike Peek, and Will Browar—my personal ghosts and demons are quite real, but so too are friends good enough to help me face them. I will always be grateful for our bond.

Thank you to Heather, my partner in all things, the love of my life. And to Riley, an unending source of wonder, laughter, frustration, and tears. My life is fuller, better, and without question more magical for sharing it with the two of you.

And finally, to my mother, as years go on, we may not be as close or in as regular contact. But you read my first forays into writing fantastical stories on the pads of gridded paper you filched from the office. You introduced me to the worlds of Star Trek and Star Wars alike and sat side-by-side to discover The X-Files, Buffy the Vampire Slayer, and other seminal texts of my youth together. Perhaps most of all, I remember you reading Analog magazines in the living room, escaping to other planes of reality, other worlds, other possibilities—impossible as they may have been. This book is for you.

JACKLEG PRESS

V. Joshua Adams * Mark Baumgartner * Scott Shibuya Brown * Michael Chin * Chloe Clark * Rivka Clifton * Brittney Corrigan * Jessica Cuello * Barbara Cully * Allison Cundiff * Curious Theatre Branch * Neil de la Flor * Genevieve DeGuzman * Suzanne Frischkorn * Victoria Garza * Reginald Gibbons * Joachim Glage * Caroline Goodwin * Brett Hanley * Kathryn Kruse * Brigitte Lewis * Jenny Magnus * DK McCutchen * Jean McGarry * Rita Mookerjee * Mamie Morgan * Alexis Orgera * Zach Powers * Karen Rigby * Jo Salas * Maureen Seaton * Kristine Snodgrass * Cornelia Spelman * Peter Stenson * Melissa Studdard * Gemini Wahhaj * Megan Weiler * David Welch * Cassandra Whitaker * David Wesley Williams

jacklegpress.org